WHITE RAT

ALSO BY GAYL JONES

FICTION

Corregidora (novel) (1975)
Eva's Man (novel) (1976)
The Healing (novel) (1998)
Mosquito (novel) (1999)
Palmares (novel) (2021)
The Birdcatcher (novel) (2022)
Butter (novellas, stories and fragments) (2023)

POETRY COLLECTIONS

Song for Anninho (1981)
The Hermit-Woman (1983)
Xarque and Other Poems (1985)
Song for Almeyda and Song for Anninho (2022)

OTHER WORKS

Chile Woman (play) (1974)
Liberating Voices: Oral Tradition in African American Literature (criticism) (1991)

WHITE RAT

Short Stories

by

Gayl Jones

BEACON PRESS
BOSTON

First published in 1977 by Random House, Inc.
Reprinted 1991 by Northeastern University Press,
by agreement with Random House, Inc.

Beacon Press
Boston, Massachusetts
www.beacon.org

Beacon Press books
are published under the auspices of
the Unitarian Universalist Association of Congregations.

Printed in the United States of America
27 26 25 24 8 7 6 5 4 3 2 1

This book is printed on acid-free paper that meets the uncoated paper
ANSI/NISO specifications for permanence as revised in 1992.

Text design and composition by Kim Arney

"The Return: A Fantasy" was first published in *Amistad 2*, edited by John A. Williams and Charles S. Harris (Random House, 1971). "Jevata" first appeared in *Essence* (Nov. 1973). "The Roundhouse" was first published in *Panache*, edited by R. B. Frank (1971). "White Rat" was originally published in *Giant Talk*, edited by Quincy Troupe and Rainer Schulte (Random House, 1975).

Names: Jones, Gayl, author.
Title: White rat : short stories / by Gayl Jones.
Description: Boston : Beacon Press, 2024. | Summary: "The acclaimed author's first collection of stories. "Gayl Jones's work represents a watershed in American literature. From a literary standpoint, her form is impeccable . . . and as a Black woman writer, her truth-telling, filled with beauty, tragedy, humor, and incisiveness, is unmatched." -Imani Perry"—Provided by publisher.
Identifiers: LCCN 2023028977 | ISBN 9780807012949 (trade paperback) | ISBN 9780807012932 (ebook)
Subjects: LCSH: African Americans—Fiction. | United States—Social life and customs—Fiction. | LCGFT: Short stories.
Classification: LCC PS3560.O483 W5 2024 | DDC 813/.54—dc23/eng/20230710
LC record available at https://lccn.loc.gov/2023028977

For Thaddeo K. Babiiha

CONTENTS

WHITE RAT

I LEARNED WHERE SHE WAS when Cousin Willie come down home and said Maggie sent for her but told her not to tell nobody where she was, especially me, but Cousin Willie come and told me anyway cause she said I was the lessen two evils and she didn't like to see Maggie stuck up in the room up there like she was. I asked her what she mean like she was. Willie said that she was pregnant by J. T. J. T. the man she run off with because she said I treat her like dirt. And now Willie say J. T. run off and left her after he got her knocked up. I asked Willie where she was. Willie said she was up in that room over Babe Lawson's. She told me not to be surprised when I saw her looking real bad. I said I wouldn't be least surprised. I asked Willie she think Maggie come back. Willie say she better.

The room was dirty and Maggie looked worser than Willie say she going to look. I knocked on the door but there weren't no answer so I just opened the door and went in and saw Maggie laying on the bed turned up against the wall. She turnt around when I come in but she didn't say nothing. I said Maggie we getting out a here. So I got the bag she brung when she run away and put all her loose things in it and just took her by the arm and brung her on home. You couldn't tell nothing was in her belly though.

I been taking care of little Henry since she been gone but he three and a half years old and ain't no trouble since he can play hisself and know what it mean when you hit him on the ass when he do something wrong.

Maggie don't say nothing when we get in the house. She just go over to little Henry. He sleeping in the front room on the couch. She go over to little Henry and bend down an kiss him on the cheek and then she ask me have I had supper and when I say Naw she go back in the kitchen and start fixing it. We sitting at the table and nobody saying nothing but I feel I got to say something.

"You can go head and have the baby," I say. "I give him my name."

I say it meaner than I want to. She just look up at me and don't say nothing. Then she say, "He ain't yours."

I say, "I know he ain't mine. But don't nobody else have to know. Even the baby. He don't even never have to know."

She just keep looking at me with her big eyes that don't say nothing, and then she say, "You know. I know."

She look down at her plate and go on eating. We don't say nothing no more and then when she get through she clear up the dishes and I just go round front and sit out on the front porch. She don't come out like she used to before she start saying I treat her like dirt, and then when I go on in the house to go to bed, she hunched up on her side, with her back to me, so I just take my clothes off and get on in the bed on my side.

Maggie a light yeller woman with chicken scratch hair. That what my mama used to call it chicken scratch hair cause she say there weren't enough hair for a chicken to scratch around in. If it weren't for her hair she look like she was a white woman, a light yeller white woman though. Anyway, when we was coming up somebody say, "Woman cover you hair if you ain't go'n' straightin' it. Look like chicken scratch." Sometime they say look like chicken shit, but they don't tell them to cover it no more, so they wear it like it is. Maggie wear hers like it is.

Me, I come from a family of white-looking niggers, some of 'em, my mama, my daddy musta been, my half daddy he weren't. Come down from the hills round Hazard, Kentucky, most of them and claimed nigger cause somebody grand-mammy way back there was. First people I know ever claim nigger, 'cept my mama say my daddy hate hoogies (up North I hear they call em honkies) worser than anybody. She say cause he look like he one hisself and then she laugh. I laugh too but I didn't know why she laugh. She say when I come, I look just like a little white rat, so tha's why some a the people I hang aroun with call me "White Rat." When little Henry come he look just like a little white rabbit, but don't nobody call him "White Rabbit" they just call him little Henry. I guess the other jus' ain't took. I tried to get them to call him little White Rabbit, but Maggie say naw, cause she say when he grow up he develop a complex, what with the problem he got already. I say what you come at me for with this a complex and then she say, Nothin, jus' something I heard on the radio on one of them edgecation morning shows. And then I say Aw. And then she say Anyway by the time he get seven or eight he probably get the pigment and be dark, cause some of her family was. So I say where I heard somewhere where the chil'ren couldn't be no darker'n the darkest of the two parent and bout the best he could do would be high yeller like she was. And then she say how her sister Lucky got the pigment when she was bout seven and come out real dark. I tell her Well y'all's daddy was dark. And she say, "Yeah." Anyway, I guess well she still think little Henry gonna get the pigment when he get to be seven or eight, and told me about all these people come out lighter'n I was and got the pigment 'fore they growed up.

Like I told you my relatives come down out of the hills and claimed nigger, but only people that believe 'em is people that got to know 'em and people that know 'em, so I usually just stay around with people I know and go in some joint over to Versailles or up to Lexington or down over in Midway where they know me cause I don't like to walk in no place where they say, "What's that white man doing in here." They probably say "yap"—that the Kentucky word for honky. Or "What that yap doing in here with that nigger woman." So I jus' keep to the places where they know me. I member when I was young me and the other niggers used to ride around in these cars and when we go to some town where they don't know "White Rat" everybody look at me like I'm some hoogie, but I don't pay them no mind. 'Cept sometime it hard not to pay em no mind cause I hate the hoogie much as they do, much as my daddy did. I drove up to this filling station one time and these other niggers drove up at the same time, they mighta even drove up a little ahead a me, but this filling station man come up to me first and bent down and said, "I wait on you first, 'fore I wait on them niggers," and then he laugh. And then I laugh and say, "You can wait on them first. I'm a nigger too." He don't say nothing. He just look at me like he thought I was crazy. I don't remember who he wait on first. But I guess he be careful next time who he say nigger to, even somebody got blond hair like me, most which done passed over anyhow. That, or the way things been go'n, go'n be trying to pass back. I member once all us was riding around one Saturday night, I must a been bout twenty-five then, close to forty now, but we was driving around, all us drunk cause it was Saturday, and Shotgun, he was driving and probably drunker'n a skunk and drunken the rest of us, hit up on this police car and the police got out and by that time Shotgun done stop, and the police come over and told all us to get out the car, and he looked us over, he didn't have to do much looking because he probably smell it before he got there, but he looked us all over and say he gonna haul us all in for being drunk and disord'ly. He say, "I'm gone haul all y'all in." And

I say, "Haul y'all all." Everybody laugh, but he don't hear me cause he over to his car ringing up the police station to have them send the wagon out. He turn his back to us cause he know we wasn goin nowhere. Didn't have to call but one man cause the only people in the whole Midway police station is Fat Dick and Skinny Dick, Buster Crab and Mr. Willie. Sometime we call Buster, Crab Face too, and Mr. Willie is John Willie, but everybody call him Mr. Willie cause the name just took. So Skinny Dick come out with the wagon and hauled us all in. So they didn't know me well as I knew them. Thought I was some hoogie jus' run around with the niggers instead of be one of them. So they put my cousin Covington, cause he dark, in the cell with Shotgun and the other niggers and they put me in the cell with the white men. So I'm drunkern a skunk and I'm yellin' let me outa here I'm a nigger too. And Crab Face say, "If you a nigger I'm a Chinee." And I keep rattling the bars and saying "Cov', they got me in here with the white men. Tell 'em I'm a nigger too," and Cov' yell back, "He a nigger too," and then they all laugh, all the niggers laugh, the hoogies they laugh too, but for a different reason, and Cov' say, "Tha's what you get for being drunk and orderly." And I say, "Put me in there with the niggers too, I'm a nigger too." And then one of the white men, he's sitting over in his corner, say, "I ain't never heard of a white man want to be a nigger. 'Cept maybe for the nigger women." So I look around at him and haul off cause I'm goin hit him and then some man grab me and say, "He keep a blade," but that don't make me no difrent and I say, "A spade don't need a blade." But then he get his friend to help hole me and then he call Crab Face to come get me out a the cage. So Crab Face come and get me out a the cage and put me in a cage by myself and say, "When you get out a here you can run around with the niggers all you want, but while you in here you ain't getting no niggers." By now I'm more sober so I jus' say, "My cousin's a nigger." And he say, "My cousin a monkey's uncle."

By that time Grandy come. Cause Cov' took his free call but didn't nobody else. Grandy's Cov's grandmama. She my grandmama too on my stepdaddy's side. Anyway, Grandy come and she say, "I want my *two* sons." And he take her over to the nigger cage and say, "Which two?" and she say, "There one of them," and points to Cov'ton. "But I don't see t'other one." And Crab Face say, "Well, if you don't see him I don't see him." Cov'ton just standing there grinning, and don't say nothing. I don't say nothing. I'm just waiting. Grandy ask, "Cov, where Rat?" Sometime she just call me Rat and leave the "White" off. Cov' say, "They put him in the cage with the white men." Crab Face standing there looking funny now. His back to me, but I figure he looking funny now. Grandy says, "Take me to my other boy, I want to see my other boy." I don't think Crab Face want her to know he thought I was white so he don't say nothing. She just standing there looking up at him cause he tall and fat and she short and fat. Crab Face finally say, "I put him in a cell by hisself cause he started a ruckus." He point over to me, and she turn and see me and frown. I'm just sitting there. She look back at Crab Face and say, "I want them both out." "That be about five dollars apiece for the both of them for disturbing the peace." That what Crab Face say. I'm sitting there thinking he a poet and don't know it. He a bad poet and don't know it. Grandy say she pay it if it take all her money, which it probably did. So the police let Cov' and me out. And Shotgun waving. Some of the others already settled. Didn't care if they got out the next day. I wouldn't a cared neither, but Grandy say she didn like to see nobody in a cage, specially her own. I say I pay her back. Cov' say he pay her back too. She say we can both pay her back if we just stay out a trouble. So we got together and pay her next week's grocery bill.

Well, that was one sperience. I had others, but like I said, now I jus' about keep to the people I know and that know me. The only other big sperience was when me and Maggie tried to get married. We went down to the courthouse and 'fore I even said a word, the man behind the glass cage look up at us and say, "Round here nigger don't marry white." I don't say nothing just standing up there looking at him and he looking like a white toad, and I'm wondering if they call him "white toad" more likely "white turd." But I just keep looking at him. Then he the one get tired a looking first and he say, "Next." I'm thinking I want to reach in that little winder and pull him right out of that little glass cage. But I don't. He say again, "Around here nigger don't marry white." I say, "I'm a nigger. Nigger marry nigger, don't they?" He just look at me like he think I'm crazy. I say, "I got rel'tives blacker'n your shit. Ain't you never heard a niggers what look like they white." He just look at me like I'm a nigger too, and tell me where to sign.

Then we get married and I bring her over here to live in this house in Huntertown ain't got but three rooms and a outhouse that's where we always lived, seems like to me, all us Hawks, cept the ones come down from the mountains way back yonder, cept they don't count no more anyway. I keep telling Maggie it get harder and harder to be a white nigger now specially since it don't count no more how much white blood you got in you, in fact, it make you worser for it. I said nowadays sted a walking around like you something special people look at you, after they find out what you are if you like me, like you some kinda bad news that you had something to do with. I tell em I aint had nothing to do with the way I come out. They ack like they like you better if you go on ahead and try to pass, cause, least then they know how to feel about you. Cept nowadays everybody want to be a nigger, or it getting that way. I tell Maggie she got it made, cause at least she got that chicken shit hair, but all she answer is, "That why you treat me like chicken shit." But tha's only since we been having our troubles.

Little Henry the cause a our troubles. I tell Maggie I ain't changed since he was borned, but she say I have. I always say I been a hard man, kind of quick-tempered. A hard man to crack like one of them walnuts. She say all it take to crack a walnut is your teeth. She say she put a walnut between her teeth and it crack not even need a hammer. So I say I'm a nigger toe nut then. I ask her if she ever seen one of them nigger toe nuts they the toughest nuts to crack. She say, "A nigger toe nut is black. A white nigger toe nut be easy to crack." Then I don't say nothing and she keep saying I changed cause I took to drink. I tell her I drink before I married her. She say then I start up again. She say she don't like it when I drink cause I'm quicker tempered than when I ain't drunk. She say I come home drunk and say things and then go sleep and then the next morning forget what I say. She won't tell me what I say. I say, "You a woman scart of words. Won't do nothing." She say she ain't scart of words. She say one of these times I might not jus' say something. I might *do* something. Short time after she say that was when she run off with J. T.

Reason I took to drink again was because little Henry was borned club-footed. I tell the truth in the beginning I blamed Maggie, cause I herited all those hill man's superstitions and nigger superstitions too, and I said she didn't do something right when she was carrying him or she did something she shouldn't oughta did or looked at something she shouldn't oughta looked at like some cows fucking or something. I'm serious. I blamed her. Little Henry come out looking like a little club-footed rabbit. Or some rabbits being birthed or something. I said there weren't never nothing like that in my family ever since we been living on this earth. And they must have come from her side. And then I said cause she had more of whatever it was in her than I had in me. And then she said that brought it all out. All that stuff I been hiding up inside me cause she said I didn't hated them hoogies like my daddy did and I just been feeling I had to live up to something he set and the onliest reason I married her was because she was the lightest and brightest nigger woman I could get and still be nigger. Once that nigger start to lay it on me she jus' kept it up till I didn't feel nothing but start to feeling what she say, and then I even told her I was leaving and she say, "What about little Henry?" And I say, "He's your nigger." And then it was like I didn't know no other word but nigger when I was going out that door.

I found some joint and went in it and just start pouring the stuff down. It weren't no nigger joint neither, it was a hoogie joint. First time in my life I ever been in a hoogie joint too, and I kept thinking a nigger woman did it. I wasn't drunk enough *not* to know what I was saying neither. I was sitting up to the bar talking to the tender. He just standing up there, wasn nothing special to him, he probably weren't even lisen cept but with one ear. I say, "I know this nigger. You know I know the niggers. (He just nod but don't say nothing.) Know them close. You know what I mean. Know them like they was my own. Know them where you s'pose to know them." I grinned at him like he was s'pose to know them too. "You know my family came down out of the hills, like they was some kind of rain gods, you know, miss'ology. What they teached you bout the Juicifer. Anyway, I knew this nigger what made hisself a priest, you know turned his white color I mean turned his white collar backwards and dressed up in a monkey suit—you get it?" He didn't get it. "Well, he made hisself a priest, but after a while he didn't want to be no priest, so he pronounced hisself." The bartender said, "Renounced." "So he 'nounced hisself and took off his turned back collar and went back to just being a plain old every day chi'lins and downhome and hamhocks and corn pone nigger. And you know what else he did? He got married. Yeah the nigger what once was a priest got married. Once took all them vows of cel'bacy come and got married. Got married so he could come." I laugh. He don't. I got evil. "Well, he come awright. He come and she come too. She come and had a baby. And you know what else?

The baby come too. Ha. No ha? The baby come out club-footed. So you know what he did? He didn't blame his wife. He blamed hisself. The nigger blamed hisself cause he said the God put a curse on him for goin' agin his vows. He said the God put a curse on him cause he took his vows of cel'bacy, which mean no fuckin,' cept everybody know what *they* do, and went agin his vows of cel'bacy and married a nigger woman so he could do what every ord'narry onery person was doing and the Lord didn't just put a curse on him. He said he could a stood that. But the Lord carried the curse clear over to the next gen'ration and put a curse on his little baby boy who didn do nothing in his whole life . . . cept come." I laugh and laugh. Then when I quit laughing I drink some more, and then when I quit drinking I talk some more. "And you know something else?" I say. This time he say, "No." I say, "I knew another priest what took the vows, only this priest was white. You wanta know what happen to him? He broke his vows same as the nigger and got married same as the nigger. And they had a baby too. Want to know what happen to him?" "What?" "He come out a nigger."

Then I get so drunk I can't go no place but home. I'm thinking it's the Hawk's house, not hers. If anybody get throwed out it's her. She the nigger. I'm goin' fool her. Throw her right *out* the bed if she in it. But then when I get home I'm the one that's fool. Cause she gone *and* little Henry gone. So I guess I just badmouthed the walls like the devil till I jus' layed down and went to sleep. The next morning little Henry come back with a neighbor woman but Maggie don't come. The woman hand over little Henry, and I ask her, "Where Maggie?" She looked at me like she think I'm the devil and say, "I don't know, but she lef' me this note to give to you." So she jus' give me the note and went. I open the note and read. She write like a chicken too, I'm thinking, chicken scratch. I read: "I run off with J. T. cause he been wanting me to run off with him and I ain't been wanting to tell now. I'm send little Henry back cause I just took him away last night cause I didn't want you to be doing nothing you regrit in the morning." So I figured she figured I got to stay sober if I got to take care of myself and little Henry. Little Henry didn't say nothing and I didn't say nothing. I just put him on in the house and let him play with hisself.

That was two months ago. I ain't take a drop since. But last night Cousin Willie come and say where Maggie was and now she moving around in the kitchen and feeding little Henry and I guess when I get up she feed me. I get up and get dressed and go in the kitchen. She say when the new baby come we see whose fault it was. J. T. blacker'n a lump of coal. Maggie keep saying "When the baby come we see who fault it was." It's two more months now that I been look at her, but I still don't see no belly change.

YOUR POEMS HAVE VERY LITTLE COLOR IN THEM

"YOUR POEMS have very little color in them, no color," she said.

"That's true," he said.

I wonder why they haven't.

The man with the beard sits in the corner of the room with his legs crossed. He's not looking at me. I want to go over and say something to him but don't know what to say.

Anyway, I don't think I should be here.

The woman who talks about Paris and the French Theatre and Sartre is very nice. She tells how cats make her nose run and she has allergies.

I can't imagine being Proust and having no one talk. I can imagine me.

(I am at a lunch table. There are eight of us. No one is talking. "What's the matter?" I ask. "No one's saying anything. Is everybody sleepy or is this just an uncommunicative time?" "It's just an uncommunicative time." "Everybody's meditating.")

But it was not an uncomfortable silence, a natural one. This was my first uncomfortable silence with him. I suppose it's because we were supposed to be talking.

A lot of people here say a lot of things, trying to be funny, and I don't know how to answer them, and end up saying what I don't mean, if anything. "All conversations are lies, or something like that." But I do not try to please.

These people are older than me except for one girl who knows me but I don't know her. She talks, and now I know her. I say how I have heard her name before and she gives me possible reasons why.

The three-and-a-half-year-old boy who is terribly brilliant is going to bed. I should have met him earlier, I think. I would have had somebody to talk to.

I listen.

The man in the corner with the beard isn't saying anything now. Once he was standing talking, once he even talked to me, but I didn't know very much to say to him.

There are two kinds of people, those who don't talk and those who can't talk.

Some people talk a lot. They are sometimes very nice people.

There are some people who can't talk or don't talk or don't know what to say. These are the people you have to get to know. They are sometimes very nice people, too.

Some people say things they shouldn't say, like Mr. B., who said a very bad thing. It is better to say nothing at all than to say what you shouldn't say.

Some people think before they talk. Some people talk before they think. Some people make you say things you don't want to say. I don't know how they do it. I wish I knew someone who could make you say what you do want to say. I suppose that is only yourself.

Some people try to be funny. Some people don't have to try to be funny. Sometimes I can be funny. Sometimes I can be ridiculous. I don't try to be funny anymore. Once I was making up funny songs and telling funny stories to the girls in the dorm. They thought they were very funny at first. But since I did it all the time and was never serious except with a few close friends, one close friend, they got tired of my funny songs and funny stories and dances. And so I am not funny anymore nor free. They were very disgusted and made me feel bad.

musterole between my toes
I had a cold
I had a cold
My mother rubbed me in musterole
I went to bed
It hurt my head
Went up my nose
When I arose
I raised my head to see my feet
For they were burning with so much heat
And I had musterole between my toes
I had musterole between my toes
Nobody knows
Nobody knows
How it got there.

"You've heard about folk saints in Mexico. How they're also called healers sometimes and go around healing people. You remember in the olden days how they tortured heretics and people who weren't what they claimed to be by putting them on the rack or hanging them from their toes. There was this folk saint named Antonio de la Vega. A Mexican folk saint, a Christ figure, and you know how when Christ was on the cross they said if you're really who you say you are why don't you save yourself. There's this record album that tells the story of the saint to go along with the song they composed about him.

They hung him from his toes
Why don't you let yourself go
You say that you're a folk saint
But you're doing things you caint
Antonio, Oh, Antonio

"Is that all? Had us sitting here listening for that?"

They all leave.

"Hangman, Hangman, slack that noose" is a real song and so is "Flat Foot Floogie with the floy floy" and so is "Make me a pallet on your floor."

And if your good girl comes
Darling she will never know
Make me oh make me a pallet on your floor
And when your good girl comes
Darling she will never know.
Now they believe nothing I tell them, even when I say I am reformed.

But this is digression. (Convenient)

There are people. They are talking. I am twenty. I used to think twenty was old. Old people are young. Young people are old. The oldest person in the room is three and a half.

There is a man whom I call "the man" who is terribly nice. He is talking to me now, or not talking. Then he says something about going. I asked him is he going. He says yes. Then I say yes. Then he and I and Mr. W. who are inseparable get in a small car, he is squeezed up in the back, but doesn't mind, and I am driven back to the campus. When I get out he starts to climb out and into the front seat. I am inside by now and a lot of girls are watching Paul Newman in *Hombre*. I go upstairs and change my clothes and come back down. I never knew so many people cared about Paul Newman. "He has beautiful eyes," someone said. He died at the end of the picture and many people were sad. "It used to be that the star of the picture always lived," Emma said. Most people go upstairs but some stay downstairs and play bid whist. I don't play cards, except poker, but nobody ever wants to play poker. So I tell them cards is a vice, the same as smoking and drinking and staying up late. The news is finally over, fortunately, and a picture comes on with some man and Mamie Van Doren. Somebody gets up to change the channel because there seems to be a general consensus that nobody wants to see Mamie Van Doren. The girl who is about to change the channel asks, "Does anybody want to see Mamie Van Doren?" I say, "I want to see Mamie Van Doren." She changes the channel anyway. There is a picture with Kirk Douglas and he is close with the Indians. He comes down by the stream and takes off his shirt and starts washing up. An Indian girl is down by the stream washing some clothes. He is older than she by many years, but she is old enough to be considered a woman, a very young woman. She seems angry with him when he comes over by her.

"You're mad at me because I saw you bathing in the stream this morning," he says. "I used to see your mother wash you when you were this high."

"I'm not that high anymore," she says.

She starts to get up, but he grabs her and kisses her, or tries to. She fights and has her knife out but he takes it away from her and she breaks away and runs back to camp.

Later he comes back into camp with his shirt still off. There is a handsome young Indian man watching him, but he is terribly silent.

Later Kirk Douglas is lying in the sand. He is throwing the knife in the sand, playing with it.

They tell me to get up and go to bed because I am going to sleep on the couch.

THE WOMEN

I WAS THREE YEARS OLD when the first woman come. My mama had just get the divorce from my daddy. Miss Maybell was the first woman. Miss Maybell Logan. She lived up on Douglas Street and had a mustache. All us children used to point at her and make fun a her cause she had a mustache. But the grownups didn't. I guess they had just got used to it. Miss Maybell Logan used to come sometimes and spend the night. I used to wonder why she come and spend the night when she got her own house. She used to go in the bedroom with mama and sleep where my daddy used to sleep. My mama always couldn't get to sleep when Miss Maybell was there, cause she be tossing and turning all night. I'd get scared sometimes and hide under the covers. When my daddy was there, in the mornings, while it was still dark outside, my mama would let me go in the bedroom and climb in the bed and sleep between the two of them. But when Miss Maybell was there, mama wouldn't let me sleep between the two of them. I was scared of Miss Maybell anyway. I didn't want to get in bed with them. In the morning, Miss Maybell would look at me with her mustache, and then she would leave. Miss Maybell kept coming till I was five, and that's how I remembered her since I was three. And then when I was five, my mama and Miss Maybell have a fight, but I didn't know what the fight was about, and then Miss Maybell didn't come no more. It was just like when my mama and daddy have the fight, and then my daddy didn't come back.

I asked my mama, "Why Miss Maybell don't come no more?"

"She a bitch's whore."

Something else happened when I was five, before Miss Maybell left. My cousin Freddie who was ten come up to stay with us three days cause his mama have to go up to Michigan for a Baptist convention. My mama put Freddie on the couch in the living room to sleep. The second night Miss Maybell come. She act like she didn't like to see Freddie there. She just look at him with her big mustache and call him "funky pants" like she call all little boys. I didn't know what she call little girls because my mama wouldn't let me hear it. She just say, "Winnie here," and Miss Maybell wouldn't call me what she was going to. Miss Maybell didn't leave cause Freddie was there. Her and my mama just went on in the bedroom and close the door. Miss Maybell just say, "Pet, I'm sleepy early." My mama name Gertrude, but Miss Maybell always call her "Pet."

Freddie grin up at Miss Maybell while she in the room but when she leave he call her "pussy woman." I ask him, "What that mean?"

"It mean she got a pussy mouth."

"What that mean?"

"It mean she a pussy willow."

"What that mean?"

"It mean what I hear my mama say. It mean she a woman that want to be a man."

"She is a man. Got whiskers."

"Naw, she got a mustache."

"Woman don't got a mustache."

"Your mama got one."

"Naw she don't."

"Only it so little you caint see it."

"Naw I caint."

"When you grow up you goin' have one."

"Naw I won't."

"Only it be so little you won't be able to see it. Just like your mama. When you grow up you gonna be jus' like your mama."

"Naw I won't."

"Live with her, don't you?"

"Yeah."

"Be like her then. My mama say you be like the company you keep."

"Then you be like your mama too."

"No, I be like my daddy."

"I ain't got a daddy."

"You got a fake fucka daddy."

"What that mean? I'ma tell."

"She be mad if you go in there."

"Then I'ma tell tomorrow."

"I be left tomorrow."

"Tell her way 'fore the cock crow."

Freddie laughed.

"Mustache Woman still be in there then. Ain't got no cock to crow."

"Miss Floyd keep chicken next door. She keep chicken and a big red rooster. He crow ev'ry morning."

"How old you?"

"Five."

Freddie didn't say nothing.

"How old are you?"

"Old enough to crow."

"I'm old enough to crow too."

Freddie laughed. "You ain't even old enough to cackle."

"I'm old enough to do what you old enough to do."

"Born 'fore you was."

"Naw you wasn't."

"My Mama Daddy did it 'fore your Mama Daddy did it."

"Did what?"

"Do what they do in there. Only ain't nothing goin' happen in there."

"What they do in there?"

"Wont me to show you?"

"Yeah. They be mad if we go in there."

"We ain't goin' in there. What y'all got in y'all's basement?"

"Nothing."

"Show me what you ain't got."

"You goin' show me what they do in there?"

"You know when we get back."

We have to go outdoors to get into the basement, and then when we get there, I ask, "You wont me to turn on the light?"

"Don't need no light."

"How we see?"

"Don't need to see. Our eyes 'just in a minute."

"What she keep in here?"

"Some old rugs over on the floor. That about all."

"Get over on the old rugs. I show you what they been doing ev'ry time she come here."

He raise my dress up and take my panties down and then he was doing something to me but I didn't know what he was doing. I wont to get away but was scared to scream cause my mama'd come down here and then Miss Maybell'd come down here and see we doing what they been doing, and then he did it. And then he put his hands down there and wipe it on my dress, but I just sit there. He say, "Cover up your ass 'fore you get a cold pussy." I pull my panties back up, and pull my dress back down and still just sit there.

"We better be going," he says.

"I don' wanna go."

"Your mama wonder where we at. If she come out the pussy room." He laugh.

"Aw'n care where we at."

He grabs me by the arm and I don't say nothing, but let him take me up the stairs with him, and he keeps saying, "They feelin' pussy, that's what they doing. They feelin' pussy. They feelin' titties. You ain't got none." Then he hush up when we go in the house. And then he say when there ain't nobody there, "See, they ain't come out the pussy room. We better go bed." Then he let my arm go. "Go bed with you if I had my own house," he says and then he go in the front room where he sleep, and I climb into bed and keep all my clothes on.

"Where Freddie?"

My mama in the kitchen cooking breakfast. Miss Maybell wa'nt there like she always wa'nt.

"His mama come and got him early."

"Aw."

"What you do to your dress?"

"Slep' in it."

"You know better'n that."

"Yes'm."

"Go take it off and I wash it. You be big enough to be going to school soon."

"I big enough to do it now. I jus' ain't old enough."

"Awright, put on your little jumper and then come and get your eggs while they still hot. Wash you up later."

I put on my jumper and then came back and eat my eggs while they still hot.

After a while, my mama said, "You quiet. What you and Freddie find to do las' night?"

"Nothing. We just go straight on to bed. Like y'all done. When his mama come get him?"

"Right after seven. He was up bright and early like he know she was coming. Maybell open the door. She always get up 'fore the cock crow. . . . You finished? You better go wash up."

"Yes m'am."

Little after that Mama and Miss Maybell have they fight. I didn't know where they have their fight, cause they couldn't had have it in the house because I never did hear them fighting, and then all a sudden, Miss Maybell just weren't coming anymore and when I ask mama, mama call Miss Maybell that bad name, and then mama didn't talk about Miss Maybell no more. Miss Maybell still live in that little house up on Douglas Street, and all us children still point at her and say, "They goes the mustache woman."

The next woman that my mama have in the house was name Fanny. Fanny Bean have pretty skin like milk and cocoa, and her hair have waves in it. I liked Fanny Bean. Fanny Bean would smile at me but never speak to me. My mama said Fanny Bean was shy. Fanny Bean was a little woman. My mama said Fanny Bean was twenty-seven and taught in school. I liked Fanny Bean. Fanny Bean was an old maid school teacher who didn't have a husband and came to live with us. That was still before I was old enough to go to school. Fanny Bean would smile at me but wouldn't talk to me. My mama said that was because Fanny Bean didn't know what to do with little children. She taught grown-up children in school. Sometime when Fanny Bean was on her way to school, she would fix my breakfast, but wouldn't talk to me. I never talk to Fanny neither, but I still like Fanny. Fanny have skin like milk and cocoa. Fanny sleep in the room where my mama sleep because my mama said there weren't enough room in the rest of the house. I didn't ask her why couldn't Fanny sleep where Freddie sleep. Fanny stayed with us till I was old enough to go to school. When I asked my mama, "Why Fanny Bean ain't here no more?" She say, "Fanny Bean a bitch's whore."

When I was old enough to go to school, my mama said she was going to work in the tobacco factory. She said now that she didn't have Fanny help pay the bills, the alimony just weren't enough, not with me starting in the first grade. I asked her why she going to work in the tobacco factory, stead of someplace else. She said she was going to work in the tobacco factory because she didn't wont to be fucking around no white woman's kitchen and she said, "If you got to work for The Man, least you can work somewhere where you don't come in contact with him personal." I asked her what she was going to do there. "Sort tobacco. Only they probably have me down there mopping till I learn what I'm s'pose to do and then they probably say I ain't learned what I'm s'pose to do when I'm s'pose to do it, just so they can keep me down there mopping. And then they have they summer layoffs. And then prob'ly the next year they have me sort tobacco."

When I started in the first grade my mama took me down to the schoolroom and then she told me to be good and then she went to the factory. The teacher take me and sit me in a chair in the back of the room cause there weren't no chairs in the front of the room, and then the teacher went up to the front of the room and ask the children what nursery rhymes they knew and then she played them on her piano and have all the children sing nursery rhymes. I didn't sing. I sit in the back beside another little girl in the back of the room.

"What your name?"

"Retta Pace."

"Winnie Flynn."

"Win Flynn."

"How come you ain't singing?"

"Don't know what they singing."

"I know what they singing. I just don't want to sing. Mama said she goin' teach the alfbet."

"Yeah."

"I know it already. Cept write it down. She teach to sing it firs."

"I don't know it."

After the teacher finished singing the nursery rhymes, she taught the children how to sing the alphabet. She have skin like milk with a little bit of tea in it. Retta Pace sing. Retta have skin like coffee with chocolate syrup in it. I didn't sing. When the teacher get through teaching them to sing the alphabet, she come to the back of the room and bend down to me.

"Why aren't you singing? Don't you know it yet?"

"I know it all ready. I want a learn how to write it down."

"I have to hear you sing it first."

"I know it all ready."

Miss Fletcher go back to the front of the room. They sing the song again but I still don't sing.

Miss Fletcher say, "Winnie will have to stay after school and sing for me."

I say to Retta, "My mama come and get me."

Miss Fletcher say, "No talking."

After school when all the desk chairs empty except mine Miss Fletcher come back to the back of the room and say, "Now will you sing."

"I want to learn what I don't already know."

"Well, then, talk them for me."

"Do you know Miss Fanny Bean up to the big school?"

"Yes, she teaches at the high school, doesn't she?"

"My mama sleep with her."

Miss Fletcher don't say nothing.

"My mama sleep with you too."

I ran out the room.

That evening a man bring my mama a note from school. It said that they have transferred me into Miss Dalton's class. She older, and more experienced with difficult children. My mama ask me what did I do wrong the first day. I say, "Nothing." My mama say I had to done something. I say, "Miss Fletcher a white lady, ain't she?" My mama say she wasn't white, she was just real light.

The next day I didn't mind being moved over into Miss Dalton's room. By that time they got off singing the alphabet and start writing it down.

The next day at recess, I see Retta standing over by the sliding board. When I come over, Retta say, "I heard you said something bad and nasty to the teacher and they put you outta school."

"They didn't put me outta school, they just move me over to some other room. What the white lady do today?"

"What white lady?"

"Miss Fletcher. I call her the white lady but mama say she ain't white, just real light."

"Nothing. She told us to bring in tablets tomorr'."

"We start writing this morning. Miss Dalton ain't even got a piano in her room. She a old lady, kinda tall, an' dark."

"Miss Fletcher the music teacher. Tha's how come she got a piano. This morning some big third-graders come in to get they music lesson."

"Aw."

"What you say to her?"

"Nothing."

"Had to been something."

"You too young to hear."

"Old as you."

"Naw you ain't."

"How old are you, Win Flynn?"

"Six."

"I be seven. Jan'ary. When you be seven?"

"'cember."

"Olderner."

"Naw y'ain't. Mama said it don't matter how old you are. What you know. She say I act old'ner some people fourteen. She call me her little lady."

"So. You prob'ly fast with boys."

"Naw ain't."

"Yes y'are."

"I said ain't."

"You see that girl over there."

"Where?"

"Girl got the good hair."

"Yeah."

"Her mama keep her and her sister locked up in the yard behind a white fence and keep a dog in the yard and won't let no boys come inside the yard. Anytime a boy come he have to stand outside the fence and talk. Her sister ten. I stand outside and fence and talk too cause I'm scared the dog."

"What's her name?"

"Bev'ly Carp'ter. She say don't like you and don't want to play with you cause she say you fas' with boys."

"How she know if I am if I ain't?"

"Cause her sister ten and your cousin Freddie 'leven and he stand up at the fence and talk."

"Tell her kiss my black ass."

"Awww."

"Why you still standing here?"

"Aw' no."

"I thought you be go tell Bev'ly what I said."

"I ain't a tattle."

"You in'cent?" I ask.

"What?"

"In'cent. You ever had a boy?"

"What?"

"Come on over here by the fence. . . . You ever had a boy put it in you?"

"Put what in me?"

"His *thing*."

"Naw."

"I bet you don't even know what being fast mean."

"Yeah I do."

"I bet you don't even know what he got that you ain't got."

"Yeah I do."

"I bet you ain't never seen it."

"Naw. But I know what it look like. Debby seen it. She got a brother. She told me what it look like. So. I bet you ain't never seen it neither."

"Naw I ain't never seen it, but I had it put in me."

"How you have it put in you an' ain't never seen it?"

"It was dark. Couldn't see nothing."

"How come?"

"I was raked when I was five. You know how they talk about on the radio how such an' such a girl get raked."

Retta laugh. "They don't say raked, they say raped."

"Thought you didn' know nothing."

"Know what I hear."

"Know what I hear. Know what I do too."

"Who raped you?"

"My cousin Freddie."

"Mama say that's call 'cest. Somebody kin to you do it to you. Say it's bad."

"Anybody do it to you bad. Thought you didn't know nothing."

"Know that."

"You in'cent?"

"I ain't never had it put in me. Seen it neither. Hear about it."

"I bet you don't even know how they put it in you. I bet you don't even know what you s'pose do."

"Naw."

"Flap your legs open just like a book. And then he put it in you."

"Your mama know?"

"Course she know. She got me. You got to do it firs."

"What you get?"

"Nothing. I ain't ol' enough. You got to have titties firs," I say.

"Debbie Allen got titties."

"That mean she been doing it all a time. Got to be leas' thirteen."

"She in the third grade."

"She ain' ol' enough."

"Your mama know you been doing it?"

"I didn't did it but once. Then I didn't do it. *He* did it."

"Your mama know he do it?"

"Naw. Cept day after she was washing clothes and come in and ask me how come my panties got blood on 'em and I say I didn' know and then she say, 'You too young to bleed' and then she don' say nothing else and then after that she just be call me her little woman."

When my mama started working in the tobacco factory, she started bringing different women home. I never get to know them because it seem like each time they was different and they would come late in the evening just about when it was my bedtime and my mama would say, "So-in-so got to stay the night cause she ain't got no place to stay tonight." I remember once some woman came and then left real quick cause I hear the woman say, "I didn't come here for this." And my mama say, "Don't you come shaking your ass at me like you got something down there I wont." And then the woman left. There was other women.

Once I ask my mama if my friend Retta from the school could stay over the weekend cause her mama was going up to Detroit to the Baptist convention. My mama say, “We ain’t got enough room.”

“She can sleep with me.”

“Your bed ain’t big enough.”

“She littler than me.”

“Well, awright.”

Retta’s mama bring her over the next Friday evening and bring her little weekend bag. Retta’s mama sat on the couch in the front room and talked for a while with my mama.

“I certainly do appreciate this Misses Flynn. I didn’t have nobody take Retta. I even got them to let me off from work, and then find ain’t nobody take Retta. All the Baptist women out the church goin’, so couldn’t get one of them. I certainly do ’preciate this.”

“Where you work?”

“Out the narcotics farm.”

“Least ain’t no white woman’s kitchen. I tell everybody stay out them white woman’s kitchen. All them addicts, though. You like it?”

“Naw, not especially. Actually, I caint stand it. At first I thought it be interesting, you know, only one of two like it in the country.”

“Other one over somewheres in Texas, ain’t it?”

“Uh-hum. You know, Billie Holiday was out to this’n.”

“Was she?”

“You know, when she was goin’ through all that stuff. Friend of mine, used to work out there ’fore I did, said she seen her too. Look real bad.”

“I can imagine.”

“Skin coming off her.”

“I can imagine.”

“I ain’t had to seen nothing like that though myself.”

“How long you been out there?”

“Six months. Work with the dieticians.”

"Yeah."

"It's this other stuff going on out there I don't like."

"What other stuff?"

"Well, they got the women se'grated from the men."

"Yeah."

"I'm in 'ere with the women. Got people standing on top of chairs and stuff. Now 'at ain't so bad. It's this other stuff got me lookin' for someplace to go. Don't mean it literally, I stay there."

"What other stuff?"

Retta's mama screw up her nose. "You know, women hugging on each other. Guess when you in a sit'ation where you ain't got nothing else, like them women in them prisons too you hear about, you get that way. But it just ain't right. I don't think it's right. Do you think it's right?"

My mama don't say nothing, she just let Retta's mama go on talking.

"Well, what got me was this one woman come up to me pulling all on me and say, 'I been trying to go wid Gertrude but Maggie go wid her. I'm scared to go up an' tell her. Can you go up and tell her I wanta go wid her too.' I just tell her I don' even know Gertrude, and try to shrug her off and go on about my business what they pay me for."

That night Retta slept in my bed with me. She was little and skinnier than me, so we fit together all right. My mama said that she woulda let one of us sleep on the couch if we wanted to but that she was entertaining some guests that night. I said we didn't mind cause Retta said her mama didn't turn all the lights out at night in they house and she was scared of the dark if she was by herself. Then my mama said, "Then it work out just fine, won't it."

"They be guest from the fact'ry?" I ask.

"Yeah. I be have two hussies over. One of them prob'ly get so drunk she 'bout down need the couch."

When me and Retta was alone and all the lights was out I ask Retta, "You scart?"

"Naw. You scart?"

"Naw. I ain't never scart a what I caint see in the dark. See it, then you be scart a it."

"I be scart a it e'n if I don't see it."

"You a scarty cat. You a scart pussy."

"What that mean?"

"Pussy another name for a woman, or a girl. Like I heard mama say to this woman, 'Pussy, don't be that way. Don't be that way, pussy.'"

"Aw."

We laughed.

"If I'da said 'You got a scart pussy' I been talking about your thing."

"Aw, *I* know it."

"You don't ack like it."

"Yeah I do. . . . What you doin'?"

"Trying to feel pussy. Let me feel it. I don' think you know what you got down there."

"Yeah I do."

"Let me feel it then."

"Okay."

It was soft and smooth with no hair on it.

"Feel good, don't it?"

"Yeah."

"Cept I ain't s'pose to be doing it."

"Why not?"

"Boy s'pose to do it."

"I wouldn't let a boy do it."

"Yeah you would."

"Naw I wouldn't."

"When you grow up."

"Don't know if I would when I grow up."

"Then you be a queer donut."

"Naw I won't."

"Yes you will."

"Naw I won't."

"I let a boy do it when I grow up. Wouldn't let a girl do it though."

"You doin' it."

"Cept we dif'rent. We *little* girls. When you git titties you ain't suppose to let a girl do it. That mean you queer. I ain't goin' be queer."

"I ain't either."

"You said you was."

"Naw I wasn't."

"Yeah. You am' goin' have nothing but pussy feelers."

"Feel yours."

"Be a pussy feeler same thing."

"Caint feel mine if I caint feel yours."

"I ain't through yet. Smooth down there. Still feel good, don't it?"

"Yeah. Wanna feel yours?"

"When you get growed, you gonna have hair all over down there."

"Naw I won't."

"Yes you will."

"Naw I won't."

"Your mama does."

"Naw she don't."

"Ast her."

"If I ast her she wouldn' tell me. She ast me who I been talkin' to."

"Mean your mama a scart pussy too."

"Why?"

"Scart to talk to her own girl child about sex."

"Naw she ain't. Told me I be bleeding down there when I got be about twelve. Told me in front a my daddy too."

"So. I been bleeded. Cept it ain't come on strong yet. I probably be bleeding 'fore you be bleeding."

"Naw you won't."

"Yeah I will."

"Debbie sister bleed. Somebody say, 'See that girl. She bleed every month.' I didn' know what they talking about. Thought it was something bad. Went home and ask my mama and tha's when she told me."

"See."

"See what?"

"Had to tell you. Wouldn't a told you if she didn' had to."

"Yeah she would."

"Naw."

"Feel yours."

"Okay."

Mine didn't have no hair on it neither.

"Feel good to your hand too, don't it?"

"Yeah."

Before Retta's mama came to get her to take her home, Retta said, "Maybe Mama let me come stay overnight with you sometime she ain't goin' up to the Baptist 'vention."

But Retta's mama never did let her come back and spend the night with me. We still was best friends at school though, until we got in the six grade and Retta and her mama and her daddy moved up to Columbus, Ohio. So we never did know who started bleeding first. I started after I was halfway through the six grade, and my mama have to put paper towel down there till she get the right sized Kotex cause I was so skinny.

When I was halfway through the six grade that was when I saw what I wasn't supposed to see. I got up in the part of the night that was close to morning to go to the jar. We didn't have a bathroom in them days and my mama kept the slop jar in a little room next to the kitchen. When I got to the little room next to the kitchen I heard some woman say, "I parked my car round to the back door."

Then I heard my mama say, "Goodnight, honey. Goodmorning, ain't it?"

Then I didn't hear nobody say nothing, and peeped around and saw my mama standing up in the back door kissing some big woman, and then I didn't go to the jar, but went on back to bed. I get under the covers and say, "I ain' goin' be like my mama when I grow up. I ain' goin' be a bitch's whore." Then I just waited till I hear the back door slam and my mama come back through the house before I go try the jar again.

It wasn't until I was fourteen that I went out on a date with my first boy. But I didn't go out with him anymore because he kept wanting to kiss me and I didn't want him to and every time he call I would say, "I'm goin' work on my science club project," and then I hang up the telephone. He had taken me to the movies and had put his arm around my shoulders so that his hand dangled down so that he could feel my titties through my clothes. I didn't know what else to do so I had let him do it.

Once after I didn't go out with him anymore I was sitting in the school cafeteria by myself. After Retta left, I didn't make anymore girl friends. Some of them tried to get friendly but I wouldn't get friendly back. When I was sitting in the cafeteria by myself this boy came over. He was chocolate-colored and had paper doll eyes. He say, "You still working on your science club project?" He grinned. He had crooked teeth. I didn't say nothing.

"Mind if I sit here?" he ask.

"Naw, it's free."

He sat down. He was heavyset, but not fat, and looked older than he was, but I knew he was just fourteen too.

"Lew said you wouldn't go to the bowling alley with him las' week cause you was working on your science club project."

"You Lew's friend, or the whole world know?"

"We hang around together sometimes."

"Aw."

"You keepin' company?"

"Keepin' yours."

"You know what I mean, you going with anybody?"

"Naw."

"Wanta keep my company? Is, if you through with your science club project."

"Turned it in."

"Well?"

"I don't know."

"You cold, ain't you?"

"Naw."

"Don't say nothin' to nobody, do you?"

"Say somethin' to me I do."

"You know Alvin Davis?"

"Yeah, he in my Citizenship class."

"He say he saw you come down the street with your head all in the air, wouldn't speak."

"Didn't see him. Air where it b'longs."

"You cute too, ain't you?"

"Naw."

"You okay. Pie all you havin'? Make you fat. Some people think just eat dessert, don't make you fat, but it do."

"Sometimes I don't even have any lunch. I just go stand down in the girl's bathroom till the lunch period over."

"You on a diet?"

"Naw."

"Mama said if you go on a diet 'fore you get grown mess you up when you get grown."

"I ain't on a diet. Sometimes a lot of people make me nervous, and then I don't know nobody to sit with."

"Sit with me. Cept you ain't said we be keeping company yet. Lot of people make me nervous too, but I just come on in sit down anyway. Don't talk to boys. Don't talk to girls neither. You kinda funny, but don't know what kind of funny."

"There's some girls that stand down in the bathroom sometimes and smoke. Sometimes I talk to them."

"You smoke?"

"Naw. You?"

"Naw. Bad for you."

"Yeah."

"Bad for you 'fore *and* after you get grown."

"Yeah."

"You talk to anybody else? I mean talk talk."

"Talk when I got somethin' to talk about."

"Talk in class?"

"Naw. Ain't got nothin' to talk about in class."

"You look like you talk in class."

"Talk when they ask me a question. Talk on the blackboard. Talk on a paper when they give a assignment."

"You okay."

I didn't say nothing. The bell rang that meant lunch period was over.

"We be keepin' company," he said.

I got up and left without saying nothing.

The next time I saw him I was sitting on the rock fence outside school. It was recess. He just come walking by. He walked over where I was. He didn't sit down.

"Sitting by yourself again," he said.

"Yeah."

"Didn't ask what your name was. Didn't tell you mine."

"Winnie Flynn."

"Garland Morton."

Then he just walked on away.

I didn't go back in the cafeteria any more because I didn't want him to come over. I didn't know why I didn't want him to. I'd stand down in the girls bathroom with the girls that smoked, and sometimes they'd talk to me. But most of the time they didn't talk to me, they just look over at me, and I look back over at them. One of the girls was dark chocolate and sixteen and looked like a woman but was in the same grade I was in. What made her look like a woman was that her hips were round and wide and she wore straight skirts. The other girl was the color of milk coffee and had long black straightened hair. Sometimes the milk coffee girl would bring her lunch down in the bathroom and eat it there, but most the times they didn't eat lunch either. The milk coffee girl looked like she knew what to do with boys, but whenever she talked to me she never talked about what she did with boys. I didn't know what we talked about after we got through talking about it. The dark chocolate girl looked like boys had been doing things to her but she didn't know what they were doing.

"Want a cigarette?" milk coffee asked.

"No thank you. I don't smoke."

"Wish I didn't." Then milk coffee smiled.

I smiled.

Milk coffee had little bumps on her face but she had a lean firm face and I thought she was pretty. She looked old too because she had a shape that made her look like a woman too. Sometimes her eyes were dark underneath even when she didn't put makeup around her eyes.

"Want to go sit outside after I smoke before the bell ring? They goin' be coming in checking the bathroom see who's smoking somebody said."

Milk coffee and dark chocolate put out their cigarettes.

"Have to start smokin' in the stalls," dark chocolate said.

"Then they see the smoke comin' up over the stall," milk coffee said.

Think you burning pussy, I thought, but didn't say it out loud.

"Just say your pussy hair caught on fire, you try'n to put it out," dark chocolate said.

Milk coffee didn't say anything. Then she said, "They ask you how it do that."

"Tell 'em you been givin' out too much pussy," I said. They looked at me like I was bad, and made me feel bad, and then milk coffee said we better go outside if we was going to go outside before the lunch bell rang. Dark chocolate said she rather stay in the bathroom. Me and milk coffee, who say her name was Shirley, went outside and sat on the rock fence till the bell rang. We didn't say anything to each other, just sat on the fence and watched the people that passed by. Then when the bell rang we went different ways to our lockers to get our books.

"You been avoiding me or somethin'?" Garland asked.

He caught up with me when I was on my way home from school.

I looked over at him but didn't say nothing.

"Saw you sitting over there with that girl today. Wouldn't speak. Get with some girl don't want to speak."

"Didn't see you. If I see you I speak."

"Where you live?"

"Breathitt."

"I live up in the project."

"Aw."

"Walk you home?"

"Guess."

"If you don't want me to, just say so, I walk over to th'other side the street."

"That be silly."

"I mean if you don't want me walk with you."

"Don't make me no difference you walk with me."

"Say it like that I just well cross over the other side."

"I didn't mean it like that. Street's free. You be walking on the street."

"Wouldn't be coming this way didn't see you."

"Aw."

"Want to go to the show Saturday?"

"What's on?"

"I don't know. Jus' ask you you wanta go. The Lyric show."

"Naw, I be busy."

"Doing what?"

"Work."

"What kind of work?"

"School work."

"Bet you ain't got enough school work go over the whole weekend."

"Do."

"I get mines done evening, through. Ain't got another science club project?"

"Naw. Other work."

"Why you don't want to go?"

"No reason."

"Scared I try something?"

"Naw. Wouldn't let you."

He grinned. "Scared you try something?"

"Naw."

"Why won't you go?"

"No reason."

"Ask why."

"Cause I don't want to. Don't like the show."

"Come visit you?"

"Mama don't like nobody come on Saturday cause she be waxing the floor."

"Come sit on your porch then."

"Don't like to sit on the porch."

"Come take you for a walk."

"Said I don't like to go nowhere much."

"Didn't."

"I don't."

"Aw, come on. You cold, you know that."

"I live over cross the street. I guess I cross over. See you around school."

"I be over there one these days, surprise you. Surprise your mama too."

I didn't say anything. I just crossed over to the other side of the street.

"Who that boy I seen you with?"

"Aw, some boy at school."

"What's his name?"

"Garland Morton."

"Any kin to John Morton?"

"Don't know."

"Used to go to school with John Morton myself. Might be his boy. Prob'ly have one about your age."

"Don't know."

"Got a lot a homework?"

"Yes m'am."

"Your supper's in there on the table. I ate mine a ready. Told Alice I be up to see her. Be back 'fore it gets dark."

"Yes m'am."

"You go on in and eat 'fore it gets cold."

"Yes m'am."

"Be bout two hours."

"Yes m'am."

Mama went out the door and I went in to get something to eat.

When I finished eating I heard a knock on the door. I didn't know who it was and wondered why whoever it was didn't ring the bell.

When I got to the door I opened it and Garland was standing out on the porch, outside the screen door. I didn't open the screen door.

"Can I come in?" he asked.

"My mama ain't home."

"What diff'rence that make?"

"I don't think she like me having nobody here, 'specially boy when she ain't at home."

"I don't see what diff'rent it makes. Aw, come on let me come in. When you spect your mama back?"

"She said she be gone two hour. That was bout a half hour ago."

"I be gone in a hour, a half hour. I just come to visit you cause you wouldn't let me visit you if I didn't come."

He started twisting the knob of the screen door, but it was locked.

I said, "Aw, awright," and opened the screen door. Garland came in.

"You got a nice house," he said.

"If you don't got to live in it."

"Your mama keep things around."

"What-nots."

"Yeah, my mama got those around too. She paint pictures and put them up on the wall. Daddy tell her take 'em down. She say she don't like look at the bare wall."

"Aw."

I sat down on the couch, and he sat down beside me.

He said, "My mama paint up all her own furniture too. She don't never keep it the same color the store got it. She always paint it up herself and call herself being creative."

"Aw."

"Give me your hand."

"Why?"

"Just want to hold your hand."

I gave him my hand.

"Got nice sof' hand. Bet you don' wash dishes."

"Yeah, I wash dishes. You?"

"Naw. Mama do. I told her I ain' goin' do what a woman do. Didn't tell her like that. She be slap the shit out a me if I did. I tell her I empty the garbage 'stead, wash down the outdoor windows or something."

"Aw."

"You know I don't mind the way you say aw. Don' want to be bothered with me, tell me to go, but don' go 'Aw' me."

"Don' have nothing to talk about."

When he put his hand on my leg I didn't say nothing. I was thinking of my mama gone to visit Miss Alice that live down the road. She probably be more than two hours.

He started feeling my leg at the knee and then moved almost up where the crotch was. My legs felt warm all inside. Then he put his hand on my crotch feeling me, and then he was kissing me and feeling me through my panties. And then he said, "Let's get out the front room."

"Where?"

"Where you sleep."

We got up and I started in my room, but changed my mind, and take him into my mama's bedroom. Then I lay down on my mama's bedspread, and let him get on top of me.

JEVATA

I DIDN'T SEE JEVATA when she ran Freddy away from her house, but Miss Johnny Cake said she had a hot poker after him, and would have killed him too, if he hadn't been faster than she was. Nobody didn't know what made her do it. I didn't know either then, and I'm over there more than anybody else is. Now I'm probably the onliest one who know what did happen—me and her boy David. Miss Johnny Cake don't even know, and it seem like she keep busier than anybody else on Green Street. People say what make Miss Johnny so busy is the Urban Renewal come and made her move out of that house she was living in for about forty years, and all she got to do now is sit out there on the porch and be busy. Once she told me she felt dislocated, and I told Jevata what she said, and Jevata said she act dislocated.

Miss Johnny Cake aint the onliest one talking about Jevata neither. All up and down Green Street they talking. They started talking when Jevata went up to Lexington and brought Freddy back with her, and they aint quit. They used to talk when I'd come down from Davis town to visit her. Then I guess they got used to me. I called myself courting her then. We been friends every since we went over to Simmons Street School together, and we stayed friends. I guess all the courting was on my side though, cause she never would have me. I still come to see about her though. I was coming to see about her all during the time that Freddy was living with her.

"I don't see what in the world that good-lookin boy see in her," Miss Johnny Cake would say. "If I was him and eighteen, I wouldn't be courting the mama, I be courting the daughter. He aint right, is he, Mr. Floyd?"

I wouldn't say anything, just stand with my right foot up on the porch while she sat rocking. She was about seventy, with her gray hair in two plaits.

"I don't see what they got in common," Miss Johnny said.

"Same thing any man and woman got in common," I said.

"Aw, Mr. Floyd, you so nasty."

Before Freddy came, Jevata used to have something to say to people, but after he came she wouldn't say nothing to nobody. She used to say I was the only one that she could trust, because the others always talked about her too much. "Always got something to say about you. Caint even go pee without them having something to say about you." She would go on by and wouldn't say nothing to nobody. People said she got stuck up with that young boy living with her. "Woman sixty-five going with a boy eighteen," some of the women would say. "You seen her going up the street, didn't you? Head all up in the air, that boy trailin behind her. Don't even look right. I be ashamed for anybody to see me trying to go with a boy like that. Look like her tiddies fallen since he came, don't it? But you know she always have been like 'at though, always looking after boys. I stopped Maurice from going down there to play. But you know if he was like anybody else he least be trying to get some from the daughter too."

Now womens can get evil about something like that. Wasn't so much that Jevata was going with Freddy, as she wouldn't say nothing to them while she was doing it. Now if she'd gone over there and said something to them, and let them all in her business and everything, they would felt all right then, and they wouldn't a got evil with her. "Rest of us got man trouble, Miss Jevata must got boy trouble," they'd laugh.

Now the boy's eighteen, but Jevata aint sixty-five though, she's fifty, cause I aint but two years older than her myself. I used to try to go with her way back when we was going to Simmons Street School together, but she wouldn't have me then, and she won't have me now. She married some nigger from Paris, Kentucky, one come out to Dixieland dance hall that time Dizzy Gillespie or Cab Calloway come out there. Name was Joe Guy. He stayed with her long enough to give her three children. Then he was gone. I was trying to go with her after he left, but she still wouldn't have me. She mighta eventually had me if he hadn't got to her, but after he got to her, seem like she wouldn't look at no mens. Onliest reason she'd look at me was because we'd been friends for so long. But first time I tried to get next to her right after he left, she said, "Shit, Floyd, me and you friends, always have been and always will be." I asked her to marry me, but she looked at me real evil. I thought she was going to tell me I could just quit coming to see her, but she didn't. After that she just wouldn't let me say nothing else about it, so I just come over there every chance I get. She got three childrens. Cynthy the oldest. She sixteen. Then she got a boy fourteen, name David, and a little boy five, name Pete. Sometime she call him Pete Junebug, sometime Little Pete.

Don't nobody know where in Lexington she went and got Freddy. Some people say she went down to the reform school they got down there and got him. It ain't that he's bad or nothing, it's just that they think something's wrong with him. I didn't know where she got him myself, because it was her business and I figured she tell me when she wanted to, and if she didn't wont to, she wouldn't.

Miss Johnny Cake lives over across the street from Jevata, and every time I pass by there, she got to call me over. Sometimes I don't even like to pass by there, but I got to. She thinks I'm going to say something about Jevata and Freddy, but I don't. I just listen to what she's got to say. After she's said her piece, sometimes she'll look at me and say, "Clarify things to me, Mr. Floyd." I figure she picked that up from Reverend Jackson, cause he's always saying, "The Lord clarified this to me, the Lord clarified that to me." I ain't clarified nothing to her yet.

"He's kinda funny, ain't he?" she said one day. That was when Freddy and Jevata was still together. It seemed like Miss Johnny Cake just be sitting out there waiting for me to come up the street, because she would never fail to call me over. Sitting up there, old seventy-year-old woman, couldn't even keep her legs together. One a the men on the street told me she been in a accident, and something happened to that muscle in her thighs, that's supposed to help you keep your legs together. I believed him till he started laughing, and then I didn't know whether to believe him or not.

"That boy just don't act right, do he? He ain't right, is he, Mr. Floyd? Something wrong with him, aint it?" She waited, but not as if she expected an answer. I guess she'd got used to me not answering. "You reckon he's funny? Naw, cause he wouldn't be with her if he was funny, would he? I guess she do something for him. She must got something he wont. God knows I don't see it. Mr. Floyd, you just stand up there and don't say nothing. Cat got your tongue, and Freddy got hers." She looked at me grinning. I blew smoke between my teeth. "If you wonted to, I bet you could tell me everything that go on in that house."

I said I couldn't.

"Well, I know she sixty-five, cause she used to live down 'ere on Poke Street when I did. She might look like she forty-five, and tell everybody she forty-five, but she ain't. Now, if that boy was *right*, he be trying to go with Cynthy anyway. That's what a *right* boy would do. But he ain't right. He don't even *look* right, do he, Mr. Floyd?"

I told her he didn't look no different from anybody else to me.

Miss Johnny grinned at me "You just don't wont to say nothin' against her, do you? Aint no reason for you to take up for him, though, cause he done cut you out, aint he?"

I said I was going across the street. She said she didn't see why I won't to take up for him, cut me out the way he did.

One day when I came down the street, Freddy was standing out in the yard, his shirt sleeves rolled up, standing up against the post, looking across the street at Miss Johnny, looking evil. I didn't think Miss Johnny would bother me this time. I waved to her and kept walking. She said, "Mr. Floyd, aint you go'n stop and have a few words with me? You got cute too?" I went over to her porch before I got a chance to say anything to Freddy. He was watching us, though. Green Street wasn't a wide street, and if she talked even a little bit as loud as she'd been talking, he would have heard.

"Nigger out there," she said, almost at a whisper. "Keep staring at me. Look at him."

She kept patting her knees. I didn't turn around to look at him. I was thinking, "He see those bloomers you got on."

"Look at him," she said, still low.

"Nice day, aint it?" I said, loud.

"Fine day," she said, loud, too, then whispered, "I wish he go in the house. I don't even like to look at him."

I said nothing. I lit a cigarette. She started rocking back and forth in her rocker, and closed her eyes, like she was in church. Or like I do when I'm in church.

"You have you a good walk?" she asked, her eyes still closed.

I said, "OK."

We were talking moderate, now.

"You a fool you know that? Walk all the way out here from Davis town, just to see that woman. She got what she need, over there."

I hoped he hadn't heard, but I knew he had. I wondered if I was in his place, if I would have come over and said something to her.

"You know you a fool, don't you?" she asked again, still looking like she was in church.

I didn't answer.

"You know you a fool, Mr. Floyd," she said. She rocked a while more then she opened her eyes.

"But I reckon you say you been a fool a long time, aint no use quit now."

I turned a little to the side so I could see out of the corner of my eye. He was still standing there. I couldn't tell if he was watching or not. I felt awkward about crossing the street now. I gave Miss Johnny a hard look before I crossed. She only smiled at me.

"Mr. Floyd," Freddy said. He always called me "Mr. Floyd." He was still looking across the street at Miss Johnny. I stood with my back to her. He asked me to walk back around the yard with him. I did. I stood with my back against the house, smoking a cigarette.

"I caint stand that old woman," he said. "You see how she was setting, didn't you? Legs all open. I never could stand womens sit up with their legs all open. 'Specially old women."

I said they told me she couldn't help it.

"I had a aunt use to do that," he said. "She can help it. She just onry. Aint nothin wrong with that muscle. She just think somebody wont to see her ass. Like my aunt. Used to think I wonted to see her ass, all the time."

I said nothing. Then I asked, "How's Jevata . . . and the children?"

"They awright. Java and Junebug in the house. Other two at school."

I finished my cigarette and was starting in the house.

"Think somebody wont to see her ass," Freddy said. He stayed out in the yard.

Jevata was in the kitchen ironing. She took in ironing for some white woman lived out on Stanley Street.

"How you, Floyd?" she asked.

"Not complaining," I said. I sat down at the kitchen table. She looked past me out in the back yard where Freddy must have still been standing.

"What Miss Busy have to say about me today?" she asked, looking back at me.

"Nothin'."

"You can tell me," she said. "I won't get hurt."

"Miss Johnny wasn't doing nothing but out there talking bout the weather," I said.

"Weather over here?" she asked.

I smiled.

She looked back out in the yard. I thought Freddy was still standing out there, but when I turned around in my seat to look, he wasn't. He must have gone back around to the front of the house.

"How you been?" she asked me as if she hadn't asked before, or didn't remember asking.

She wasn't looking at me, but I nodded.

"I never did think I be doing this," she said. "You 'member that time I told you Joe and me went down to Yazoo, Mississippi, and this ole, white woman come up to me and asked me did I iron, and I said, 'Naw, I don't iron.' I wasn't gonna iron for *her*, anyway."

I said nothing. I had already offered to help Jevata out with money, but she wouldn't let me. I worked with horses and had enough left over to help. Now, I was thinking, she had *four* kids to take care of.

"He found a job yet?" I asked.

She looked at me, irritated. She was sweating from the heat. "I told him he could take his time. He aint been here long. He need time to get adjusted."

I was wondering how much adjusting did he need. It was over half a year ago since she went and got him.

"You don't think Freddy's evil, do you?" she asked.

I looked at her. I didn't know why she asked that. I said, "Naw, I don't think he's evil." She went back to ironing. I just sat there in the kitchen, watching her. After a while Freddy came in through the back door. He didn't say anything. He passed by, and I saw him put his hand on her waist. She smiled but didn't turn around to look at him. He went on into the front of the house. I sat there about fifteen or twenty minutes longer, and then I got up and said I was going.

"Glad you stopped by," Jevata said.

I said I'd probably be back by sometime next week, then I went out the back way.

Miss Johnny not only caught me when I was coming to see Jevata, but she caught me when I was leaving.

"I never did think that bastard go in the house," she said. "Sometime I wish the Urban Renewal come and move me away from here. They dislocate me once, they might as well do it again."

I was thinking she probably heard Reverend Jackson say, "When the devil dislocate you, the Lord relocate you."

"How's Miss Jevata doing?" she asked.

"She's awright," I said.

"Awright as you can be with a nigger like that on your hands. If it was me, I be ashamed for anybody see me in the street with him. If he wont to go with somebody, he ought to go with Cynthy. I didn't tell you what I seen them doing last night?"

"What?" I asked frowning.

"I seen 'em standing in the door. Standing right up in the door kissing. Thought nobody couldn't see 'em with the light off. But you know how you can see in people's houses. Tha's the only time I seen 'em though. But still if they gonna do something like that, they ought to go back in there where caint nobody see 'em, and do it. Cause 'at aint right. Double sin as old as she is. And they sinned again, cause you spose to go in your closet and do stuff like that."

I said nothing.

"You know I'm right, Mr. Floyd."

I still said nothing.

"Naw, you prob'ly don't know if I'm right or not," she said.

I looked away from her, over across the street at Jevata's house.

"Tiddies all sinking in," she said. "I don't see what he see in her. Look like she aint got no tiddies no more. I don't see what he see in her. You think I'm crazy, don't you? I just don't like to see no old womens trying to go with young boys like that. I guess y'all ripe at that age, though, aint you?"

I said I couldn't remember back that far.

"Floyd, you just a nigger. You just mad cause you been trying to go with her yourself. I bet you thought y'all *was* going together, didn't you? Everybody else thought so too, but not me. I didn't."

I turned around to look at her. She kept watching me.

"Aint no use you saying nothing neither, cause I know you wasn't. I can tell when a man getting it and when he aint."

I started to tell her I could tell when a woman wonts it and can't have it, but I just told her I'd be seeing her.

"You got a long walk back to Davis town, aint you, Mr. Floyd?"

The next time I was down to Jevata's only the girl was at home. I asked her where her mama was. She said she and Freddy took

Junebug downtown to get him some shoes. She told me Jevata had been mad all morning.

"Mad about what?" I asked.

"Mad cause Miss Johnny told Freddy to go up to the store for her."

"To get what?"

"A bottle of Pepsi Cola."

"Did he go?"

"Naw, he sent Davey." Then she said, "I don't know what makes that woman so meddlesome, anyway."

We were in the living room. I hadn't set down when I heard Jevata wasn't there. She was still standing, her arms folded like she was cold. She was frowning.

"What is it?" I asked.

"I guess I do know why she so meddlesome, why they all so meddlesome," she said.

I waited for her to go on.

"They talking about them, aint they, Mr. Floyd? People all up and down the street talking, aint they?" She didn't ask the question as if she expected an answer. She was still looking at me, frowning. She was a big girl for sixteen. She could've passed for eighteen. And she acted older than she was. She acted about twenty.

"Sometimes I'm ashamed to go to school. Kids on this street been telling everybody up at school. But you know I wouldn't tell mama. I don't wont to hurt her. I wouldn't do anything to hurt her."

I was thinking Jevata probably already knew, or guessed that people who didn't even know her might be talking about her.

I didn't say anything.

"They saying nasty things," she said.

I still didn't say anything. She kept looking at me. I put my hand on her shoulder. She was the reason I understood how Jevata could feel about Freddy, those times I felt attracted to Cynthy, wanting to touch those big breasts. I took my hand away.

"Just keep trying not to hurt her," I said.

She was looking down at the floor. I kept watching her breasts. They were bigger than her mama's. I was thinking of Mose Mason, who they put out of church for messing with that little girl him and his wife adopted. The deacons came to the house and he said, "I aint doing nothing but feeling around on her tiddies. I aint doing nothin' y'all wouldn't do." They was mad, too. "They ack like they aint never wont to feel on nobody," Moses told me when we was sitting over in Tiger's Inn. "Shit, I bet they do more feeling Saturday night than it take me a whole damn week to do. And then they come sit up under the pulpit on Sunday morning and play like they hands aint never touched nothin' but the Holy Bible. Saying amen louder than anybody. Shit, don't make me no difference, though, whether I'm with 'em or not cause the Baptist is sneaky, anyway. Sneak around and do they dirt."

"I can hear them," Cynthy said quietly. "I can hear her telling him to hold her. 'Hold me, Freddy,' she say. I can hear her telling him he's better to her than my daddy was."

I couldn't think of anything to tell her. I wanted to touch her again, but didn't dare.

When Jevata came in, she said, "Cynthy tell you what that bitch did?"

I nodded.

"I know what she wonts, bitch," she said. "I know just what she wonts with him."

She asked me if I wanted something to eat. I said, Naw, I'd better be going. I'd been just waiting around to see her.

"Why did she try to kill 'im, Mr. Floyd?" Miss Johnny asked. It was a couple of weeks after Jevata had gone after Freddy with the poker.

"I don't know," I said. I had my right foot up on the porch and was leaning on my knee, smoking.

"Got after Cynthy, didn't he? I bet that's what he did."

"He didn't bother Cynthy," I said, angry. But I didn't know whether he did or not.

"I bet tha's what he did. I bet she went somewhere and come back and found them in that house." She started laughing.

"I don't know what happened," I said.

"Seem like she tell you, if she tell anybody," Miss Johnny said.

I threw my cigarette down on the ground and mashed it out.

"I wish she let me come over there and get some dandelions like I used to, so I can make me some wine out of 'em," she said.

"If Freddy was over there, you could tell him to get you some," I said.

"I wouldn't tell 'at nigger to do nothing for me," she said. She was angry. I looked at her for a moment, and then I walked out of the yard.

When I got to Jevata's, she was sitting in the front room with her housecoat on, the same dirty yellow one Cynthy said she was wearing the day she threatened to kill Freddy. Cynthy said she hadn't been out of the house since she chased Freddy out. I asked her if she was all right.

"Aint complaining, am I?" she said. She said she had some Old Crow back there in the kitchen if I wanted some. I said, "Naw, thank you." She hadn't been drinking any herself, which surprised me. She didn't drink much anyway, but I thought maybe with Freddy gone, she might.

"Shit, Floyd, why you looking at me like that?" she asked.

"I didn't know I was looking at you any way," I said.

"Well, you was."

I said nothing.

"I seen Miss Bitch call you over there. What she wont this time?"

"She wonts to know why," I said.

"I aint told *you* why."

"And you won't, will you?"

She looked away from me, then she said, "You know it always have took me a long time, Floyd."

She didn't say anything else, and I tried not to look at her the way I had been looking. She sat on the edge of the couch with her hands together, like she was nervous, or praying. Her shoulders were pulled together in a way that made her look like she didn't have any breasts.

Cynthy came in the front room, and asked me how I was.

"Awright."

"Mama, supper's ready," she said.

"Stay for supper, won't you, Floyd?" Jevata asked me.

"Yeah."

"Cynthy, where's Freddy?" Jevata asked suddenly.

Cynthy looked at me quickly, then back at Jevata.

"He's not here, Mama," Cynthy said.

"Floyd, you aint seen Freddy, have you?" Jevata asked me.

I just looked at her. I couldn't even have replied as calmly as Cynthy had managed to. I just kept looking at her. Jevata laughed suddenly, a quick, nervous laugh, then said, "Naw, y'all, I don't mean Freddy, I mean where's Little Pete, y'all. I don't mean Freddy. I feel like a fool now."

I said nothing.

"He's down the road playing with Ralph," Cynthy said.

"Well, tell him to come on up here and get his supper."

"What about David, Mama?"

"You take his plate in there to him. I don't wont to see him."

"Yes, m'am."

I looked at Cynthy, puzzled, then I said I would take it. Jevata looked at me, but said nothing.

David was lying on the bed. I set his plate down on the chair by the bed. He didn't say anything.

"You know something about this, don't you?" I asked.

He still said nothing.

"I b'lieve you know what happened."

"Go way and leave me alone!" David said. "You aint my daddy."

I stood looking at him for a moment. He still lay on his belly. He had half turned around when he was hollering, but he hadn't looked at me. I finally left the room. When I came back in the kitchen, Little Pete was sitting at the table and Cynthy was putting the food on the table.

"Where's Jevata?" I asked.

Cynthy said nothing.

"I just ask her when Freddy was coming back and then she start acting all funny. I didn't do nothin', Mr. Floyd."

"I know you didn't," I said.

Cynthy looked at me and sat my plate down on the table. I sat down with them. Jevata didn't come back.

"Don't you think you better take your mama a plate," I said to Cynthy.

"She said she didn't wont nothin'," she said.

I stood up.

"She looked like she didn't wont nothin', Mr. Floyd," Cynthy said.

I sat back down.

I knew there was one place I could find out where Freddy was. I took the bus to Lexington, then went over to the barber shop over in Charlotte Court, right off Georgetown Street.

"Any y'all know Freddy Coleman?" I asked.

They didn't answer. Then, one man sitting up in the chair, getting his hair trimmed around the sides, cause he didn't have any in the top, said, "What you got to do with him?"

"Nothin'," I said. "I just wont to know where he is."

"I used to know. He used to keep the yard down here at Kentucky Village."

Some of the other men started laughing. Kentucky Village was a school for delinquent boys. I asked what was funny.

"Close to them KV boys, wasn't he," one of the men said.

The man in the chair started laughing. "He never did do nothing. Just used to stand up there with the rake. Womens be passing by looking. Didn't do 'em no good." He asked me why I wanted him.

"I'm just looking for him," I said.

They looked at each other, like people who got a secret. They were trying not to laugh again.

"You can try that liquor store up the street. They tell me his baby hang out over there."

The rest of the men started laughing. I left them and went up to the liquor store. Somebody told me Freddy was living in an apartment up over some restaurant off Second Street.

I found the place and went upstairs and knocked on the door. He wasn't glad to see me.

"How you find me?" he asked.

I came in before he asked me to. I stayed standing.

"What do you wont?" he asked. "Finding out where I am for *her*?"

"Naw, for myself," I said.

I looked around. The living room was small. Only a couch and a couple of chairs, and a low coffee table. On the coffee table was a hat with feathers on it. It was a woman's hat. We were both standing. I didn't sit down without him asking me to. He wasn't saying anything and I wasn't. I was thinking he *was* a good-looking man, almost *too* good-looking. The onliest other man I knew was *that* good-looking was Mr. Pindar, a fake preacher that used to go around stealing people's money. He used to get drunks off the street and have them go before the congregation and play like he had changed their life. And people would believe it, too. He was so good-looking the women would believe it, and preached so good the men would believe it.

Freddy kept standing there looking at me. I kept looking at him.

"Where's my ostrich hat?" It was a man's voice, but somehow it didn't sound like a man.

Freddy looked embarrassed, he was frowning. He hollered he didn't know where it was.

"You seen my ostrich hat, honey?" the man asked again. He came in, like he was swaying, saw me and stopped cold. He said, "How do," snatched the hat from the table and went back in the other room.

Freddy wasn't looking at me. I said I'd better be going.

"He's crazy," Freddy said quickly. "He live down at Eastern State, and he's crazy."

Eastern State was the mental hospital.

"He got a room down at Eastern State," Freddy said. "They let him out every day so he can get hisself drunk. That's all he do is get hisself drunk."

I said nothing. The man had come back in the room, and was standing near the door, pouting, his lower lip stuck out. Freddy hadn't turned to see him.

I started to go. Freddy reached out to put his hand on my arm, but didn't. He looked like he didn't want me to go.

"I was going to ask you to come back to her," I said, my eyes hard now. I ignored the man standing there, pouting. "I was going to tell you she needs you."

Freddy looked like he wanted to cry. "You know she kill me if I go back there," he said.

"Why?" I asked.

He said nothing.

I went toward the door again and he came with me. He still hadn't turned around to see the man. I asked him why again. Then I wanted another why. I asked him why did he go with her in the first place.

He said nothing for a long time, then he reached out to touch my arm again. I don't know if he would have stopped again this time, but I stood away from him.

"She was going to the carnival. You know the one they have back behind Douglas Park every year, the one back there. She was passing through Douglas Park and seen me sitting up there all by myself. She ask me if I wont to go to the carnival. I don't know why she did. Maybe she thought I was lonesome, but I wasn't. I was sitting up there all by myself. She took me with her, you know. They had this man in this tent who was swallowing swords and knives, you know like they do. She wanted to take me there, so I went. We was standing up there watching this man, up close to him. We was standing up close to each other too, and then all a sudden Miss Jevata kind of turned her head to me, you know, and said kind of quiet like, 'You know, Miss Jevata could teach you how to swallow lightning,' she said. That was all she said. She didn't say nothing else and she didn't say that no more. I don't even know if anybody else heard her. But I think that's why I went back with her. That was the reason I went with her."

I said nothing. When I closed the door, I heard something hit the wall.

"Freddy did something to David, didn't he?" I asked her.

"Naw, it wasn't David," Jevata said. She was sitting with her hands together.

I frowned, watching her.

"Petie come and told me Freddy tried to throw him down the toilet. I didn't believe him."

"If he tried he would've," I said. "What did him and David do?"

She kept looking at me. I was waiting.

"I seen him go in the toilet," she said finally. "Him and David went back in the toilet together. He didn't even have his pants zipped up when he come back to the house."

I was over by her when she burst out crying. When she stopped, she asked me if I could do something for her. I told her all she had to do was ask. When she told me she still loved Freddy, that she wanted me to get him back for her, I walked out the door.

I thought I wouldn't see her again. When the farm I worked for wanted me to go up to New Hampshire for a year to help train some horses, I went. I told myself when I did come back, I was through going out there, but I didn't keep my promise to myself.

When I got there, Miss Johnny wasn't sitting out on her porch, but Jevata was sitting out on hers—with a baby, sitting between her breasts. She was tickling the baby and laughing. When she looked up at me, she was still laughing.

"Floyd, Freddy back," she said. "Freddy come back."

I didn't know what to say to her. I asked if Cynthy was at home. She said yes. I went in the house. Cynthy was standing in the living room. She must have seen me coming.

"Freddy back?" I asked.

She put her hands to her mouth and drew me toward the kitchen.

"Naw, she mean the baby," she said. "She named the baby Freddy."

"Is it his?" I asked.

She hesitated, frowning, then she said, "Yes." She got farther into the kitchen and I went with her.

"She didn't wont to have him at first. At first she tried to get rid of him."

I kept looking at her. She was a grown woman now. I remembered when I first started coming there, right after her daddy left. Every time I'd come, she'd get the broom and start sweeping around my feet, like she was trying to sweep me out of the house. Now she looked at me, still frowning, but I could tell she was glad to see me. She said she knew I'd been sending them the money, but Jevata thought Freddy had.

I said nothing. I stood there for a moment, then I said I'd better be going.

"You will come back to see us?" she asked quickly, apprehensively. "We've missed you."

I looked at her. I started to move toward her, then I realized that she meant I might be able to help Jevata.

"Yes, I'll be back," I said.

She smiled. I went out the door.

"You little duck, you little duck, Freddy, you little duck," Jevata said, tickling the baby, who was laughing. A pretty child.

"You be back to see us, won't you, Floyd?" she asked when I started down the porch.

"Yes," I said, without turning around to look at her.

ASYLUM

WHEN THE DOCTOR COMING? When I'm getting examined? They don't say nothing all these white nurses. They walk around in cardboard shoes and grin in my face. They take me in this little room and sit me up on a table and tell me to take my clothes off. I tell them I won't take them off till the doctor come.

Then one of them says to the other, You want to go get the orderly?

She might hurt herself.

Not me, I won't get hurt.

Then they go out and this big black woman comes in to look after me. They sent her in because they think I will behave around her. I do. I just sit there and don't say nothing. She acts like she's scared. She stands next to the door.

You know, I don't belong here, I start to say, but don't. I just watch her standing up there.

The doctor will come in to see you in a few minutes, she says.

I nod my head. They're going to give me a physical examination first. I'm up on the table but I'm not going to take my clothes off. All I want them to do is examine my head. Ain't nothing wrong with my body.

The woman standing at the door looks like somebody I know. She thinks I'm crazy, so I don't tell her she looks like somebody I know. I don't say nothing. I know one thing. He ain't examining me down there. He can examine me anywhere else he wants to, but he ain't touching me down there.

The doctor's coming. You can go to the bathroom and empty your bladder and take your clothes off and put this on.

I already emptied my bladder. The reason they got me here is my little nephew's teacher come and I run and got the slop jar and put it in the middle of the floor. That's why my sister's daughter had me put in here.

I take my clothes off but I leave my bloomers on cause he ain't examining me down there.

The doctor sticks his head in the door.

I see we got a panty problem.

I say, Yes, and it's gonna stay.

He comes in and looks down in my mouth and up in my nose and looks in my ears. He feels my breasts and my belly to see if I got any lumps. He starts to take off my bloomers.

I ain't got nothing down there for you.

His nose turns red. I stare at the black woman who's trying not to laugh. He puts a leather thing on my arm and tightens it. He takes blood out of my arm.

I get dressed and the big nurse goes with me down the hall. She doesn't talk. She doesn't smile. Another white man is sitting behind a desk. He is skinny and about my age and he attaches some things to my head and tells me to lay down. I lay down and see all the crooked lines come out. I stare at circles and squares and numbers and move them around and look at little words and put them together anyway I want to, then they tell me to sit down and talk about anything I want to.

How I do?

I can't tell you that, but we can tell you're an intelligent person even though you didn't have a lot of formal education.

How can you tell?

He doesn't say nothing. Then he asks, Do you know why they brought you here?

I peed in front of Tony's teacher.

Did you have a reason?

I just wanted to.

You didn't have a reason?

I wanted to.

What grade is Tony in?

The first.

Did you do it in front of the little boy?

Yeah, he was there.

He doesn't comment. He just writes it all down. He says tomorrow they are going to have me write words down, but now they are going to let me go to bed early because I have had a long day.

It ain't as long as it could've been.

What do you mean?

I look at his blue eyes. I say nothing. He acts nervous. He tells the nurse to take me to my room. She takes me by the arm. I tell her I can walk. She lets my arm go and walks with me to some other room.

Why did you do it when the teacher came?

She just sit on her ass and fuck all day and it ain't with herself.

I write that down because I know they ain't going to know what I'm talking about. I write down whatever comes into my mind. I write down some things that after I get up I don't remember.

We think you're sociable and won't hurt anybody and so we're going to put you on this floor. You can walk around and go to the sun room without too much supervision. You'll have your sessions every week. You'll mostly talk to me, and I'll have you write things down every day. We'll discuss that.

I'll be in school.

He says nothing. I watch him write something down in a book. He thinks I don't know what he put. He thinks I can't read upside down. He writes about my sexual amorality because I wouldn't let that other doctor see my pussy.

My niece comes to visit me. I have been here a week. She acts nervous and asks me how I'm feeling. I say I'm feeling real fine except every time I go sit down on the toilet this long black rubbery thing comes out a my bowls. It looks like a snake and it scares me. I think it's something they give me in my food.

She screws up her face. She doesn't know what to say. I have scared her and she doesn't come back. It has been over a month and she ain't been back. She wrote me a letter though to tell me that Tony wanted to come and see me but they don't allow children in the building.

I don't bother nobody and they don't bother me. They put me up on the table a few more times but I still don't let him look at me down there. Last night I dreamed I got real slender and turned white like chalk and my hair got real long and the black woman she helped them strap me down because the doctor said he had to look at me down there and he pulled this big black rubbery thing look like a snake out of my pussy and I broke the stirrups and jumped right off the table and I look at the big black nurse and she done turned chalk white too and she tells me to come to her because they are going to examine my head again. I'm scared of her because she looks like the devil, but I come anyway, holding my slop jar.

If the sounds fit put them here.

They don't fit.

How does this word sound?

What?

Dark? Warm? Soft?
Me?
He puts down: libido concentrated on herself.
What does this word make you feel?
Nothing.
You should tell me what you are thinking?
Is that the only way I can be freed?

PERSONA

I HEARD THE YOUNG GIRLS TALK. I heard what they said of me. "It seems as if some man would marry Miss King. She's a nice woman."

They were freshmen. Nice girls. They were walking into town and I picked them up. The pretty one rode beside me, the other one near the door. The one beside me was not talking. The other one was asking me question after question about the school. And other things.

"I'm reading a book on women in prisons. Tonight they're showing a movie about it."

"That's for Professor Gant's class?" I asked.

"Yes. I find social psychology really interesting. I think I might major in it. . . . My mother wouldn't understand."

"Why wouldn't she want you to major in social psychology?"

"Oh, I don't mean that. I mean in my mother's day they didn't have classes like that. Professor Gant talks so openly. Doesn't she, Gretta?"

Gretta nodded, but said nothing. I looked at her a moment, then back at the road. I smiled a bit.

"If she knew what we talked about, she'd take me out of school."

I said nothing. I looked over at Gretta. She was looking straight ahead.

"It isn't anything *bad*, but she speaks so openly."

When they were where they wanted to go, I said goodbye. It was Gretta I looked at, the large dark eyes. I wanted to know if I would see her again. Yes, of course I'd see her again. But I wanted to invite her home to talk, to have dinner with me. I wanted to *see* her again. They got out of the car and were running somewhere. Her thick dark straightened hair. Her thin waist. I pulled off. I should have asked if I could pick them up, how long they'd be in town.

At the freshman lecture the psychiatrist told them they would experience sexual ambiguity here—that they would be uncertain about their womanhood. But it was natural, she said, they should not worry, most would feel it, attachments to each other, the process of growing up. They'd break away. Many young girls thought they were . . . worried about their sexuality but . . . they should not worry. Things would even out.

Did you like her?

Yes.

It is nothing to worry about. Many young women have doubts that way.

What do you mean?

It's a perfectly natural thing. You shouldn't feel like there's something wrong. You'll grow out of it.

Then I told him: I went to a woman doctor. She felt my breasts. I didn't want her to examine me there. She felt my breasts. And under my armpits. And . . . I couldn't help the way I felt when she put her hands there. A dark-haired lovely woman. She was pregnant. That made me feel tender toward her. She was very gentle and I . . . It was so strange. Then I went back to her. I kept going back to her.

They were going up the walk to the assembly building for the convocation. I kept behind them, watching the back of her head, then her waist, her broad hips.

"Do you believe in segregated schools?" her friend asked.

"What?" she said quickly. I could feel her jump.

"The separation of men and women?"

"Oh. I thought you meant . . . Where I come from it means something else."

"Oh, no! I didn't mean that."

They were silent.

"I like Miss King," she said. Not Gretta. "She's nice, don't you think? I can't understand why some man hasn't married her. She's really pretty too. In her own way."

I cut across the lawn to go in from another door, afraid one of them would turn and see me, afraid of our embarrassment, afraid it might be Gretta.

Gretta? That's a strange name for a girl from the South. She's a violet. Or a sunflower. Or a chinaberry. I sat in the back row of the auditorium where I could see everyone.

"The lecture she gave those girls. I just stood there and smiled."

I sat in the booth, saying nothing, looking at the small woman with the short hair and handsome eyes. Jean Gant. I stirred my coffee and set the spoon down.

"You'd think by now they'd do away with that lecture."

I said nothing.

"What do you think?"

"What?"

"What do you think about it?"

"Oh, I don't know."

I invited the girls to dinner. The pretty one stood behind her friend and then they entered. The pretty one, Gretta, was silent, uncomfortable. I wanted to say something, to get her talking, but . . .

"You have a lot of old books," her friend said. "Are you a collector?"

"No. Most of them were given to me. Most of the really nice ones."

"You know I didn't want to come here. To the school, I mean. I didn't want to come to an all-girls school but my parents made me. They're supposed to be the best schools." She laughed. "When I said 'segregated school' to Gretta she thought I meant like the ones they have down South."

"Gretta, have you ever been to this part of the country before?"

"No."

"Would you like more mushrooms?"

"Thank you."

She handed me her plate. I spooned on mushrooms, gave it back.

"I can't understand Eliot," her friend was saying. "I can understand Frost. I have Mrs. Justice for the poetry class. She's a good teacher, but . . ."

I looked at Gretta. She was saying nothing.

"What?" I asked her friend.

"He's so neutral . . . sexually, I mean. Even his love poems are neutral. How can anyone write intellectual love poems? Neuter love poems. That's what they are. . . . I've still got to get used to this place."

"Would you like some wine, Gretta?"

"No, I don't drink."

She kept her hands in her lap. Her knees were tight together. She looked at me, at the piano, at the pictures on the wall, the fireplace.

"I'd like some."

"What?"

"Some wine."

"Oh, I'm sorry." I got the wine, poured her and myself a drink.

"You have a fireplace," she said.

"Yes."

"It's nice to have a fireplace. We have one, but it's artificial."

"It's a luxury," I said. "One of the few I allow myself."

Why did I say that? I got up and went into the kitchen for dishes of ice cream. The one who followed me back was not Gretta.

She stood near me as I scooped ice cream out.

"You have a really nice place," she said. "It's really nice."

"Thank you."

"I'd like to have an apartment. It's a pain living in a dorm."

"I thought it was good when I was a student—meeting so many different people."

"But the upperclassmen think freshmen are fools. Women, I should say."

"What?"

"Upperclasswomen."

"Oh."

"I didn't want to come here."

"What about the classes? You said you liked Professor Gant's class."

"Yeah, the classes are okay. Hers is anyway. Academically I don't have any complaints, but . . ."

"Maybe you'll learn to like it here. The first year anyplace takes adjustments. Even if you were at a coeducational college there'd be a lot of adjustments to make."

"Yeah."

I lifted the tray. She took it from me and carried it to the living room. I got a plate of cookies. As I came in she was saying, "I don't think you act like a child." What had Gretta asked? She saw me and frowned. I set the cookies on the coffee table, and sat down, watching her.

"When I first saw you, you acted very reserved and serious, but I liked you. . . . You don't think Gretta acts like a child, do you, Miss King?"

"No."

She put her arm around Gretta. Gretta looked away from her and me. She was frowning. I wanted to say, "You're making her uncomfortable," but that would have sounded . . . patronizing?

"Gretta and I went over to one of the mixers."

"How was it?"

"It makes you feel like cattle. It's so unnatural. Men and women shouldn't have to meet like that. It's not like that in the real world."

I smiled. I started to say something, but didn't. I looked at Gretta. She was staring down at her bowl of ice cream. I felt like going over and taking her friend's arm away, pushing her away.

"Gretta handles herself real cool though. This man came over and started talking to her. Finally he looked real funny and then left. What did you say to him?"

"Nothing. He said he had to speak to somebody and just left."

"You probably said something to him you just don't want to tell."

Gretta said nothing.

"Let Gretta eat her ice cream."

"Oh."

She patted Gretta's shoulder, pushed away and picked up her bowl. When we finished, I watched her take Gretta's bowl and then mine and go out. I sat for a moment watching Gretta act uncomfortable, starting to say, "This must be a new world for you." I said nothing. Then I heard water running and went back to the kitchen.

"I'll do the dishes," she said smiling.

"No, leave them."

"I won't feel right if I don't."

I stared at the side of her face, then her back, then the dishcloths.

"You go sit down," she said. "I'll do them."

I went back into the living room. Gretta was in the same place. I'd expected her to be standing, looking at the books or pictures. I wanted to say something. I still did not know what. Her knees were so close together.

"I haven't really talked with you tonight," I said.

She looked at me. She smiled a little.

"It's always hard the first year," I said. "Every new experience is hard, and then you get used to it."

I waited. She didn't speak. I stood. "Excuse me," I said.

She looked at me, confused. I went into the kitchen. Her friend, Susan, turned to me and smiled. I took a dishtowel to dry.

"I have to do a critical paper on him," she said after a moment. She'd said something before that I hadn't heard.

"Who?"

"Eliot."

"I'm going to call it 'An Alternative to Loneliness.'"

"What?"

"The paper."

"Yes, I know. But what do you mean?"

"When I read him I have the feeling he doesn't know what to do with women."

"Who?"

She turned. I looked at her.

"I just get the feeling he wouldn't know what to do with a woman."

I stared at her invisible bosom. She was tall and straight-legged, her hair short and curly, long in the front.

"I just don't get the feeling he would know what to do. He might sleep with a woman, but just sleep."

"Has she spoken to you about persona?"

"What?"

"Has your teacher talked to you about persona?"

"Oh, yes."

I looked at her. I didn't know how my eyes were. I didn't know if she saw my look.

"I like your wooden table," she said.

I said, "Thank you."

Then I looked away from her. I started drying the pans.

"Why don't you go and sit with your friend?" I asked.

"Oh, Gretta. She's just like that. At first I thought she didn't like me. I liked her, but I thought she didn't like me. But that's just her way. She's just like that."

I took another dishtowel down from the rack, hung up the soggy one.

"She's all right when you get to know her," she said.

I started to dry the skillet but put it down.

"I'll leave these," I said. I turned back to her.

She brushed her hair back from her forehead. Her eyes were bright.

"I'll take the two of you home," I said.

"The dorms aren't far."

"But it's no good this time of night."

She shrugged, then she said, "Gretta and I were coming home last night. We went to get a pizza. There were these men at this filling station. They thought we were whores. Even Gretta doesn't look like a whore."

"Why did you say 'even'?" I stared at her.

"Well, you know . . ." She looked embarrassed, turned aside.

"Well, you shouldn't go out too much at night," I said. "The men . . . they didn't bother you, did they?" I said it like an afterthought.

"No, they just said some things. But I can't see why a woman shouldn't go ahead and do what she wants to do. I mean, you shouldn't keep yourself from doing things, going places. Nobody should take *risks*. But you shouldn't *not* do things just because you're a woman."

I said nothing. She looked at me a moment, smiling. She told me I looked tired. I smiled but still said nothing.

I let Susan off first, and then I drove Gretta back to her dorm. Gretta turned to me. "Thank you for the dinner," she said.

"When will I see you again?" I asked. My voice was almost too low to hear.

"Whenever you want to," she said. Her voice too was quiet. I couldn't see her eyes. She turned away from me. I stared at the back of her head.

I held her shoulders, then both her hands.

"You're nice," she said. "You still hide yourself too much though. . . . When I first met you, you'd be sitting there, you'd be talking and friendly but you'd never really say anything personal and it was like you'd disappeared. But other times, I was mesmerized."

She held the small of my back.

"Do you remember that lecture Dr. Hunt gave my freshman year?"

"Yes, of course."

I waited for her to say something.

"I was just thinking about it," she said.

I touched the back of her head.

"Have you seen Gretta?" she asked.

"No."

I took my hand away.

"I saw her yesterday. She acted like she didn't know me. She's started wearing her hair all over her head, like a revolutionary. They say some of the students wanted to take over one of the dorms to turn it into a black house. The chaplain spoke to them about their missing out on all the other people they have things in common with. That they shouldn't restrict their own humanity that way. One of them said the church always was the enemy. . . . I can't understand why they give so much shit about it. I can understand it, but . . ."

"Was she one of them?" I asked too quickly.

She stared at me.

"Were you in love with her? Did she ever come here?"

I didn't answer. I felt far away.

"I used to be shaped like her," she said. "And then I had gallstones taken out, and I lost my hips." She took her arms from me, holding herself.

I stared at her. She looked as if she didn't see me. I put my hand in her short hair and made her look at me.

THE COKE FACTORY

My name is Ricky. My mamas name is Ali. We live out east end on Race Street across the street from Sharlies beauty shop. My real mamas name is Willie Bean, my papa I call Papa bean but he says he aint my real papa. Anyway Ali took me when I was borned cause my real mama she had too many children and Ali she didnt couldnt have none so my mama give me to her. So we live on Race Street right down from the Freez and Elis drugstore that she send me up to sometime to get things they sell more than medcines and scriptions. She used to go over to the beauty shop but now she start to do her hair herself. I'm fifteen. She say when I get eighteent she gon to sent me out to eatern state that the mentle hospital over on forth street near the tractor place and cross the street from the liquer store. She tookt me out there one time to have me examed but they said I was too bad to learn. But they didn't want to do with me. She sat that theyd hav to put me out there when I was eightheen because that's where they put all the mently tarded after they dont hav nothing to do with them in the schol. She said shes gon have them comit me and then shes gon back to the country to live because she cant stand it here.

Yesterday she tooked me down to my mamas and said she was going to give me back to my mamas and she put all my clothes in my winter coat and tied the arms up and my mama said she didnt want me and closed the door fast and then my mama Ali said she didnt like people that didnt know how to say thank. She sat she been my mama for fifteen years and wasnt and now my real mama didnt want to take me back and she said she didnt have no legle way not to she said she could go down to the lece station and have them make her take me back. But then we just come on home. And Ali said I treat her badder than all the husbands she used to have put to gether.

We ate lunch. And she had meneggs all over her moth.

So I turnt on the television and she turnt it off and I turnt it back on and she turnt it off and said she didnt want to have to have it on all night like I had it on all night the las night when she had to sleep and get up in the morning and go to work. And then some woman next door call Fany come and she said I cant sleep he wont let me sleep he got the telvision gon on all night. He dont sleep in the night time he just watch the T.V. and then he sleep all day. And the woman lookt at me and shooked her head and I tell her woman get out and she look at my mama Ali and didnt and then I went over and open the door and pushed her out and she tell my Ali I aint comin back here no more and now when she see my Ali she dont speak cause she scart of me and she cross over on the other side of the street.

I dont go to scholl because they say they cant teach me so I walk on the street and I get cola coka bottles and take them down to the Hunns store and the Hunn gives me cans of cola when I get enough and I save them to drink and I save the cans and Ali dont like it because I kep them up on the t. v. and the t. v. in the front room but dont nobody come no more cause only women came and I didnt like them and beat them up so she keeps the shades down cause she dont want nobody to see in the livin room where I sleep.

So when it was Chrisman Alis cousin Maggie Hardy came and brought me a box of candy and I dint know it was for me and I sat is this for me and she said yes and she gave my Ali some white panties and stocking.

So I tooked my candy back in the room where Ali sleep at night so they could talkt in the front and then I here my Ali say, "I cant stand it. They laid us off at the factry but as soon as I get up enought Im goin back to the country. You know Im still payin taxes down ther so I can go back when Im ready. His mama wont take him you know they can make her take him. Im sorry its such a mes in here he keep it like that. He dont keep nothing cleaned. When I had my too husbands didnt none of em treat me like he do. You see how he do. I try to slep at night and cant cause he got the television on. And they done laid me off at the factry. You know hes retarted dont you and they don't allow him at school no more."

And then her cousin sat they dont with a question and my Ali sat no.

"His mama woodnt take him" said my Ali. "Woodnt have nothing to do with him. He's hers. They can make her take him. He fifteen now. When he gets eiteen Im jus gona put him in the mentle hospital let the state have him, right down there in the sylum. Im going back down to the country to live."

I am sit down on the floor eating the canty it was covered with choclot and white sweet stuff in the inside and a red chairy.

My Alis cousin dont anser. When I know she is gon I run in the front room and nock the coke cans off the T.V. They hit up against the grate and roll on the floor making nois and under the cot and my Ali halls off to hit me but I runned out the back way and she hollers Ricky you basterd come back here you son of a bitch. But I grabt my botle basket from the back porch and runned down the cut off and turn up Ohio and she did not come after me.

I go ferther than I been gone. When I walk up Hawkins alley two men stand clos to gether and one has a bottle that is almos empty and I walkt by them slow waiting for him to throw it down but when he finish it he hold his head back and open his moth and hold the botle up and let the whisk drip into his moth and then when ther is no more to drip he stick his tong up in the botle hole and they turnt and saw me. I grinned and then I backt up. And the one with the bottle start out after me and the other dont.

The other sat, “Aw, the boys got bad teeth.”

And the other sat, “Yeah,” and start on back.

And then I runt.

I tookt the botles down to the Hunns and that Fany was stanting up buying something and saw me. She put her pakage in front of her and backt out the store.

She said to the Hunn, “Hes a bad boy. Oh, hes bad.”

The Hunn tooked my empties and give me my coke cola.

THE RETURN: A FANTASY

JOSEPH AND MY BROTHER STEVEN were loners the first year of college. They met the second year and liked each other and started going around together. Steven would invade Joseph's room and they would read books aloud and discuss things. Steven was tall with long feet. His favorite saint was St. Martin Perez, the black Peruvian, and his favorite writer was Kafka—after he had outgrown Joyce's *Portrait of the Artist as a Young Man*. He had never gotten through *Ulysses*. Joseph was two or three inches shorter than Steven, about five foot ten. He had been a follower of Mohammed and before that Jesus, and was a journalism major at a Midwestern college before he came East and got interested in religion. He had a mustache and Steven said he still wore a belly band just because he liked the feel of it. He was thin and went in for Yoga. He was serious in his pursuit of the mysteries, and had learned to do many things with his mind and body, Steven said. Steven was unofficially majoring in everything.

I met Joseph shortly after Steven did. I went into the snack shop one afternoon, and Steven was sitting with a young man who wore dark pants and a gray sweater. His hair grew high on his forehead and he had large dark eyes, and a half-smile. He had a beard in those days. I went over to say hello to Steven. When he didn't introduce us, I said, "I'm Dora, Steven's sister."

"Joseph Corey," he answered, but neither he nor Steven said anything else to me, so I left. Joseph Corey would call on me sometimes and we would go out together, but hardly ever would the three of us be together. When Steven and Joseph were together, I felt my entrances intrusions, and Steven seemed to feel that way too. Even Joseph could be cold at these times. So I had learned to simply wave and go my way.

I remember the first time I had invaded the sacristy. It was the second time I saw them together, before Joseph had gone out with me. I went into the snack shop, got a glass of milk, and went over to where they were sitting. It was a corner table away from the jukebox. They were talking and Steven had his Kafka reader with him, and they said nothing to me when I sat down. I drank my milk, listening, but not entering into *Metamorphosis* or *The Castle*. When I finished the milk, I noticed that Steven's coffee cup was empty. Since I was going to get more milk, I asked, "Would you care for some more coffee, Steven?"

He stopped talking, looked at me. "No thank you," he said. Then he took his Kafka reader and went out.

Joseph remained, but said nothing. I noticed his empty cup and started to take it along with my glass.

"I have to go, Eudora," he said. He touched my shoulder, got up, and went out. He walked fast, as if he wanted to catch up with Steven.

After that Joseph started taking me out sometimes. I thought it was to make up for his rudeness. We went to Chinese restaurants and sat in the chapel when there was no one there, or went for walks.

Once we were sitting in a Chinese restaurant over shrimp and rice. He had moved his plate aside and was sitting with his elbows on the table, his hands folded, leaning forward.

"And that's why he had to resort to a world of fantasy," he said. "For him the fantastic became a painful reality."

He stopped talking and looked at me, not that he hadn't before, but now it was the looking and not the words he was concerned with.

"I don't like Kafka," he said.

"Why not?"

"He wouldn't like me."

"Why do you say that?"

"Steven's very brilliant," he said, as if that were the answer to my question.

"I know."

"Are you ready?"

"Yes."

Joseph paid the bill and we went outside. The restaurant was not very far from the campus, so we walked back.

"The man became a bug," he said. "Men can become bugs. There's no *as if.* You don't conduct your life *as if* you were Christ. You become Christ."

He talked on as if he were talking to himself and not me. When we passed the chapel, he said we would go inside. It was not a suggestion, but a statement of will. "We'll go in here," he said.

We went up the concrete steps, through the big door, and down the stairs on the left to the chapel basement. Along the walls of the narrow corridor were student paintings. We passed the chapel library. There was no one inside. It was almost one o'clock. We turned left again into a little backroom. There was an old harpsichord. Joseph sat down and played a sad, unrecognizable tune. When he finished, he stood up. I asked him what it was.

"Something I made up," he said.

He walked past me toward the door, then stopped and turned around.

"Are you coming?" he asked. He was strangely expressionless, and there was the air of having performed some kind of ritual.

"Are you coming?" he repeated. I went over to him and as we were going out the door, Steven was coming down the hallway. I was puzzled by what had happened and didn't say anything. Joseph said nothing. We stopped.

"Hello," Steven said. "I heard the music. I was upstairs in the pews, studying. It's a quiet place, usually. Not many people around."

"We'll see you later," Joseph said with unusual acidity. He walked past Steven. I went with him.

When we were outside and had walked a little way, he took my arm slightly. "Dora, you don't mind going the rest of the way alone?"

"No," I said, somewhat bewildered.

He left me and went back toward the chapel.

I didn't see Joseph until a couple of nights afterwards. I had just come into the snack shop where he and Steven had been talking, and Joseph grabbed my arm and invited me over.

"Did I tell you I want you to come to my place for supper tonight—you and Steven?" he asked.

"No," I uttered.

Then we were over by Steven, and he pulled out a chair for me to sit down.

"What's the occasion?" I asked.

He seemed irritated by the question, but smiled. "No occasion. I just felt like having my two best friends—"

"Your only friends," Steven inserted.

"—over for supper," Joseph went on as if he had not been interrupted.

"You've no food," Steven said.

"I can get some. Don't worry. I'll take care of everything. Come at eight." He patted my shoulder and nodded goodbye to Steven.

Joseph lived in a ragged building downtown—a little apartment building squeezed between a shoe store and a Chinese restaurant. He had lived on campus until he had been restricted. Steven said he would have fits of depression and take off whenever he wanted. He said he would lock himself in his room and not come out for days, except when he had to. The fits of depression weren't so bad. He never bothered anybody then. You just walked by and saw his door closed, and he never came out to say things to anybody. At first they had thought he was a grind, but then somebody had invaded his room by mistake and found him burning candles and meditating. Then they thought he was a mystic. No, the fits of depression weren't so bad. It was the fits of excitement, when he'd go running down the corridors in bare feet, knocking on everybody's door, and screaming in strange tongues. When he was little, he had done a lot of traveling with his father along the Mediterranean and to Oriental places. Steven said all this was just hearsay and I needn't believe it. He said I would like Joseph's place if I hadn't already been there.

At a quarter to eight Steven came by and we drove a couple of blocks downtown. As we were still ten minutes early Steven drove around the block several times; then we got out of the car and walked into a dirty anteroom and up some steep wooden stairs. Steven told me to be careful because one of the steps was broken. We turned right, down a narrow corridor to the room at the end of the hallway. Steven knocked on the door. Joseph was very happy to see us and motioned eagerly for us to come in. The room was small, rectangular. Opposite the door was a window. In the right corner, a bed covered with a brown blanket. On the right wall there were frameless inks of Chinese landscapes. There was a slender couch against the right wall, and along the left, cushions. And while the one side of the room was serenely Chinese, the other was disparate. There was a picture of a leaning cross—Jesus-less. An omnipotent eye at the top looked on a multitude below—a multitude of outstretched hands. It was not done in oil. He had cut out pictures from magazines and pasted them on canvas. That was a hobby of his. He said it represented his idea of religion.

There was a low round table in front of the couch, upon which was a tray of olives, cucumbers and dried fruit. There was a bottle of red wine, several loaves of bread and some cheese. Candles were placed at strategic points in the room—on the round table, on the window sill, on a slender table by the bed. He told us to sit down. "The couch is the only decent place." Then he offered us wine. He sliced the bread and told us to take what we liked. Then he went and sat down on one of the cushions, with his legs folded under him and the glass of wine in his hand. He said he was very glad we came.

Each time I sat my glass down, whether or not it was empty, he would rush over and fill it up again. I said he needn't bother. He said wine always tasted better when it touched the brim.

When he saw I had eaten nothing, he came over to the table and started putting cheese and olives between two pieces of bread.

"How's the wine?" he asked.

"Quite good," I said. "Thank you."

"Will you partake half with me?" he asked.

"Okay."

He cut the sandwich in half and handed part to me. Then he went back to the cushion and folded his legs under him. He looked at me for a long time. Steven had tasted neither bread nor wine. He sat watching Joseph.

"And you, Steven. Will you not partake with me? Will you not drink my wine? Will you not break bread with me?"

Steven said nothing.

"Will you not drink wine when it is especially offered you?" Joseph asked, but something foreign had suddenly come over Steven. He sat a stranger, saying nothing, watching Joseph who had offered him wine. I understood nothing of what was going on. Then

Steven got up to go. I was suddenly very disgusted with him. He asked if I was coming. I said I could find my way back. I did not like him very much then.

"Steven," Joseph called.

Steven was at the door. He did not answer. He went out.

"What's going on?" I asked. "What's between you two?"

"The cup is dead," he replied.

"I don't understand you."

"I am not come into the world to be understood. I am come to save. I am come to be believed upon."

"What about Steven?"

"He has taken the night upon himself."

I sat watching the strange slender man who sat with his legs folded under him, sipping wine and speaking in strange tongues.

"What would you do if I said I wanted to be alone?" he asked suddenly.

"I'd go."

"And not be angry?"

"No."

"I want to be alone."

"Good night, Joseph."

I went outside and stopped at a restaurant to have something very cold, and then walked back to the university.

"I haven't seen Joseph for a long time, Steve," I said. Steven looked up from his malted milk. "Where is he?"

"Probably joined some Moorish monastery."

"People don't join monasteries anymore."

"Joseph would. Even a Moorish one." He grinned.

"He hasn't locked himself in his room?" I asked, half-seriously.

"He's not there," Steven said.

"Why would he just leave?" I asked. "He was acting very strange that last night, wasn't he?"

Steven said he was.

"By the way, I've taken over his apartment," he said.

"That means he's not coming back?"

"I don't know. If he does, I'm not leaving."

Joseph's absence worried me. Steven was living in Joe's room and sometimes I would go there. He said he knew why I was depressed. He said I was in love with Joseph.

On the way back to campus one night, I passed the chapel and went inside, and downstairs to the basement, where the little room that had the harpsichord was. I sat down and started fingering it. Then I felt someone in the room with me. I looked up and Joseph was standing in the corner with his arms folded.

"Joe!" I cried. I ran over to him. "Where've you been?"

"In jail."

"Jail?"

"Not really a jail," he explained. "Apparently I ran away from my apartment that night in my pilgrim's robe. I was picked up by some cops and taken to Southern State, the mental hospital, on LSD charges until they discovered I was a manic-depressive. They said they'd let me go on a seventy-five-dollar bond, for disturbing the peace. I didn't have the money, so I stayed there."

"Why didn't you call someone?"

"I called Steven."

"He never told me. Why didn't he send you the money?"

"He said he was broke. I told him not to bother you."

Joseph looked at me the way he had that night, strangely, intently, and then he took both my arms, tightly, almost harshly.

"You know what happens to me. I go through changes. Mental changes. Manic-depressive fits. You've never seen one of them, have you?"

I said I hadn't. I said he was hurting me. He relaxed. Then he pulled me closer to him and kissed me hard. I had my hand against his chest. I said he was hurting me again.

"Hurt you into marrying me?" he asked.

I said I would marry him because I loved him.

He laughed lowly and was suddenly very gentle, and ran his fingers along my back. I said we would go tell Steven. He kissed my neck.

We were married, and stayed in Joseph's apartment, downtown, for a while. Then we moved away, first to the city, and then to a house in the country that had been Joseph's father's. Steven took over the apartment again. For the first few months there were no serious problems with Joseph. He took pills a lot, and remained tranquilized a good deal of the time. He played farmer, and worked sometimes as a private tutor. We never heard from Steven in all these months. He had come to the wedding for my sake, he said; he had never been very enthusiastic about it, even to the point of trying to talk me out of it the night before. I told him I could handle my life. He told me I would have to. I had heard recently that he had dropped most of his courses, and was raging against academia. He never answered any of my letters. He called to say hello, and to congratulate us after six months of marriage, and then I didn't hear from him for another six months.

The tales of Joseph's meditations were true. Each day he went through some new ritual, or some new bodily contortion. Sometimes, he would put on the ihram, the Moslem pilgrim's robe. He wrapped one piece of cloth around the loin and placed the other over his shoulder. He placed little bricks on the carpet, and knelt down and touched them with his forehead. He also had a long robe that he wore on special occasions. He would never let me enter into these rituals. And once, when I asked if he would teach one to me, he said simply, "You cannot do it." He seemed very serious and often secretive on these occasions, but there was no reason to doubt his sanity. Once, however, he went through a whole day and said absolutely nothing to me and wouldn't even look at me. He ate no food. Afterwards, he said it was a purification ritual.

He meditated nightly, but never longer than an hour. Then one night he went into the bedroom and stayed so long that I fell asleep on the couch. The next day he had still not come out, so I knocked on the door. There was no answer. I opened it. He was standing in front of the east window mumbling something. When he saw me, he ran to me and clung to my knees and said, "Enfold me in my mantle." He carried a blanket in his hand, so I knelt down and embraced him. In hysteria, he told me the vision. He said a tall black man had come to him, playing the trumpet. He said he was the Angel Gabriel and he carried a chain. He said he stood up the whole night praying, and that I had saved him from eternal damnation.

By evening, he was out of his mania and sitting quietly. He usually had milk at night, before he went to bed, and the tray was beside his chair. His hands were folded together under his chin and he hadn't touched the milk.

"Don't you want your milk, Joe?" I asked.

He didn't answer.

"Joseph?"

Now I said nothing. I sat down. He would drink his milk when he wanted to.

Now he turned to me and said quietly, "Don't you want your milk, Joey? No thank you." Then he stood up. "Coming, Dora?" he inquired.

"I'll be up in a few minutes," I said. "I want to take these things in the kitchen, and straighten up a bit down here, then I'll be up."

I kissed him, and he went upstairs and I took the tray into the kitchen. When I came back into the living room, I could hear him upstairs in the bathroom. I telephoned. When I was going upstairs, he was on his way down.

"What is it, Joseph?" I asked.

"I want you with me," he said. He put his arm around my waist. We went upstairs.

I brought him a glass of water from the bathroom and gave him his pill. He lay down in the bed and I sat up beside him. He stroked my back with his hand for a while, and then he fell asleep. I turned out the light and lay down. I would wake him late tomorrow.

The doctor said that he had treated Joseph before, when the police had brought him there. He said he was a very intelligent young man.

"They often are," he added.

"Who?"

"Schizophrenics."

"I thought he was a manic-depressive."

"The two symptoms often appear together. I wanted to keep him then, but there was no legal way."

"What do you mean?"

"No one to sign him in. His father couldn't be located, and we didn't know he was married."

"He wasn't married then. His father. I don't know anything about him. Joe never talks about him. He was very angry, so angry when I asked. I didn't ask again."

"He should be committed," he said.

"I couldn't do it," I said. "I love him."

"That's precisely why you should. He needs that love more than ever now."

"I don't consider that a show of love," I said.

"You will."

I got up to go.

"You think about it, Mrs. Corey," he said. "We'll talk again."

I went outside.

Schizophrenia. Two people. And sometimes becoming childlike, incoherent. I wrote a letter to Steven. I asked him what he thought I should do. A few days later I got a brief note from him. He told me to do whatever I had to. He said that I was handling my own life now.

"Joseph, where is your father?" I asked the next time we were together. "You never told me about him."

He looked at me angrily, and I thought he would say nothing.

"I don't like him very much."

"Why not?"

"He didn't like me."

That night he was very high. He kept running around the room and up and down stairs, making anonymous telephone calls and using indecent language.

I emptied some tranquilizer powders into his nightly milk and brought it to him. He was sitting in his chair, breathing hard. I was surprised when he gave me no difficulty and drank it. He said he was very tired and went upstairs to bed.

That night he had his second vision. He woke up screaming and said Gabriel had chained his right hand to his neck and his left hand behind his back.

When the men came for him, he made no resistance. He was very quiet.

"Am I out of my mind, now?" he asked.

"I think so, Joseph," I said.

He let them take him away.

Visiting day was Thursday. Steven turned up the collar of my coat against the cold. We passed through the iron gates. I told Steven it was good of him to come. He said he was my brother.

"Am I right, Steve?"

"You had to come," he said. "You love him, don't you?"

"Yes, but sometimes . . . can't I just remember him as he was before?"

"You didn't know him before."

"How I imagined he was before."

"You don't love him then."

"What do you mean?"

"He's what he is now, too. You can't divorce him from what he is now."

"If we went away, Steve . . . Can't we go away, Steven?"

"I don't know. Can we?"

We came up the stone steps and passed through the big door. There was a clean hall and people in white coats. The place was well-lighted. Steve went up to the nurse behind the desk.

"Joseph Corey," he said. "This is his wife. I'm her brother."

"Are the both of you going up?" the nurse asked.

"No. She's going up alone."

I looked at him.

"I'll wait for you here," he said. "He wouldn't want me there."

"What about me?"

"He wouldn't want me there."

"Room 212," the nurse said.

I took the stairs instead of the elevator.

I knocked on the door.

"Come in," a voice said. It was not Joseph's. I went in. Joseph was sitting in a straight-back chair by the window. The doctor was with him.

"Try not to upset him," the doctor said.

Joseph turned from the window. His beard was gone.

"Ayesha," he said quietly. I remember he had told me once that Ayesha was Mohammed's favorite wife.

"I'm not Ayesha, Joe."

"Maybe the Madonna?" he smiled. It was a weak smile. I didn't know what it meant. It was his secret.

The doctor said he would leave us alone for a while. He went out and I walked over to Joseph. He bent his head down and closed his eyes. Then he raised his head.

"I'm Eudora, Joseph," I said gently.

"I know," he replied. "Eudora taught me to pray."

I met the doctor as I was coming out the door.

"I'm going to take him with me," I said.

"I think it would be a mistake," he said. "A very serious mistake. Here he gets the very best professional care."

"He's been here two years," I said.

"Not very much is known about schizophrenia, but . . . if you expect him to get well at all . . ."

"I'll take him home," I said, not belligerently.

He shrugged. "All right."

I started away, then stopped. "You know, you can save by love," I said.

He didn't answer.

Steven was waiting for me when I got back.

"I'm taking Joe home, Steve."

"What did the doctor say?"

"He thinks Joe's ready."

"Are you ready?"

"I don't know. He wants to come. He wants to come, Steven. And he loves me."

Steven smiled.

"I'll be in the car," he said.

"Okay."

Joseph sat hunched in the corner, silent, on the way back. Neither Steven nor I said anything. Finally, we drove up to the house.

"I'm not coming in, Dora," Steven said. "I'll see you tonight."

"But . . ."

"So long, Joseph."

"Steve."

Joseph and I got out of the car, and Steven drove away.

We walked up to the house. I had left the door unlocked, so I wouldn't have to fumble with a key. I wanted everything to go smoothly.

"Do you think you'll like it here, Joe?"

"I used to live here," he said.

"Yes, I know, but . . ."

We went inside.

"If it's cold, I'll light the fire."

"It's quite comfortable, Dora, don't bother."

"All right, Joe."

I hung the coats in the closet.

"Sit down, Joe. We can talk."

"Yes—we haven't talked for a while, have we?"

We sat down.

"Steven's decided to go back to school full time," I said.

"I'm glad."

"I think things will go well for him now."

"That's good."

"Are you sure you're not cold?"

"Quite sure."

"I'll make some coffee."

"It wasn't bad there."

"What?"

"It wasn't bad there. You needn't feel guilty. It wasn't bad there at all."

"Joe, I'm . . ."

"You needn't be sorry either. You see, you mustn't ever be sorry. There's fine people there, you know. Very fine people. You mustn't ever be sorry for something like that."

"All right, Joe."

"And Dora . . ."

"Yes."

"Let's not be like the others."

"What do you mean?"

"Don't not say things. It's worse not saying things."

"What kind of wine do you want for dinner?"

Joseph said he wanted a very dry wine.

There was no dry wine, only a bottle of sweet Sauterne. I was glad when Steven came and brought the Burgundy.

"So you're going back to college full time," Joseph said. We sat at the small table in the kitchen.

"Yes."

"You've changed."

"We've all changed."

"You especially. You were the one who'd given up the academic world as hopeless."

Steven had said he would be like the Chinese artist who locked himself in his studio and hung the sign "Dumb" on the door outside, and made weird noises and pulled his hair out.

"I don't think any of us keep our Dadaistic proclamations very long."

"I thought *you* would."

"How about our having coffee in the living room?" I asked.

"Things have a way of settling themselves," Steven said.

"People have a way of forcing settlements."

"I'm sure it'll be more comfortable in the living room. Go on in. I'll bring the coffee."

Steven and Joseph went into the living room.

"Have you thought about what you'll do?" Steven was asking when I came in with the tray and set it on the coffee table.

"Joe doesn't have to think about that now, Steven."

"Yes, I've thought about it. I've thought about going back to my old job at the university."

Steven burst out laughing.

"Steven!" I exclaimed.

"I'll tell you, Joe," Steven was saying, "you don't look much like a librarian."

"Joe was not a librarian. He only sorted books for the library."

"You're making it worse, Dora," Steven said.

"Steven, I think you'd better go."

"Joe doesn't want me to go, do you Joe? We haven't talked about old times. You can't deprive two buddies of talking about old times. Those were the days, huh, Joe? Funny how you can look back at three years ago and it looks like a lifetime. Anyway, looks like a hell of a long time. How've things been?"

"Not bad. Not bad at all. I was telling Dora . . ."

"Steven, black?"

"What?"

"Do you want your coffee black?"

"You know how I like my coffee."

"I've forgotten."

"Black, and two lumps."

"And you, Joe?"

"Nothing for me, thank you. I've given up coffee."

"No coffee!" Steven exclaimed. "We used to sit up half the night drinking coffee over Kafka."

"I've given up a lot of vices of three years ago," Joseph said.

"I suppose you don't smoke anymore."

"Yes, I still smoke."

"Have a cigarette, then." Steven took out his leather cigarette case and offered him one. He offered the lighter. Joseph lit the cigarette and took a few puffs.

"That's better," Steven said. "It's good to know you're not totally corrupted. . . . Three years, seems like a hell of a long time."

"You'll be going back in a couple of weeks," I said.

"What? Back three years?" Steven asked.

"No. You know what I mean. To the university."

"I wish I could go back three years," Steven said. "As for the university, I've been back, just not full time. There're a lot of changes, Joe. A lot more Jesuses around. You were a bit too early, Joe. They don't put guys away for things like that anymore. Tell me. Did they have much trouble with you there?"

"What kind of trouble?"

"Running down the corridors in one of your rages."

"There were guards."

"That didn't seem to stop you here. They must have had less trouble with you in one of your fits of depression when you locked yourself in your room."

"We weren't allowed keys to our rooms."

"When you wouldn't come out."

"People seldom came out."

"When I hadn't heard from you a year after you were married, Dora wrote and told me how things were going with you. Wrote and told me how things were going really bad. Asked me what she should do. I told her to do whatever she had to. She told me how you used to kneel down on a bunch of bricks."

"Touch them with my forehead," Joseph corrected. "It was an act of prostration."

"She told me how she was having a hell of a time with you."

"I didn't use that word, Steven."

"A really bad time with you." Steven suddenly laughed out loud. "You must have looked like the devil in that eye-ram. The loincloth. Whatever you call it."

"Ihram. The pilgrim's robe. Two pieces of cloth. One goes around the loin, the other over the shoulder."

"Dora said you put on the eye-ram and placed little bricks on the carpet in front of you and knelt down and touched them with your forehead. After that you had your vision. Do you remember your vision, Joe?"

"I saw a black man blowing a trumpet. He was Gabriel and he carried a chain."

"That has something to do with damnation, doesn't it?"

"Yes. In the Moslem religion. If the right hand is chained to the neck, and the left hand behind the back, one is damned—eternally."

Steven grinned.

"It was after my second vision that Dora had me committed," Joseph said calmly.

"What was that?" Steven asked.

"Gabriel had chained my right hand to my neck and my left hand behind my back," Joseph replied coolly.

"Well, anyway, you must have been a hell of a sight. You shoulda took pictures, Dora—for the family album."

"We haven't a family album."

"Haven't a family album!" Steven declared. "What about the children, Dora? So your children can see their papa as a young man. Don't you want your children to see their daddy as a young man? Oh, you don't have any children. When are you going to have children, Dora?"

"Steven, I think you've said quite enough."

"I've only begun, Dora. I'm verbose, you know. I've really said very little. It just seems like a lot."

"You always were verbose, Steven," Joseph said. "When we used to hold those discussions over Kafka, you never could quite make your point. What is your point, Steven? You don't still hold a grudge after three years?"

"Hold a grudge? Of course not."

"You know Steven's too big to hold a grudge," I said. "Just because you always won out in those little sessions of yours, that's no reason for Steven to hold a grudge. He's too big a person for that. He says so himself."

"Since we seem to be throwing things at each other, you're not exempt, Dora. What about when we were over to Joseph's for supper? I left early. They told me at the dorm you didn't get back until after hours."

"You'd taken the car, and I had a hell of a time getting back."

"His place's only a couple of blocks from the university."

"I wasn't that late, Steven."

"I was worried, Dora. Don't snap at me. I just wanted to know how you made out. . . . I mean, my taking the car and all. That was very inconsiderate of me, don't you think?"

"Very."

"I'd like some more Burgundy," Joseph said. "It was quite good."

"Yes, I remember it was your favorite," Steven was saying as I went out. "Those little communions you used to hold in your room. Offering your guests bread and wine. You really knew how to play the part, didn't you, Joe?"

Steven followed me into the kitchen.

"What are you trying to do?" I asked. "Send him back?"

Steven said that wasn't a bad idea. He said he didn't think Joseph was really cured. He said why let him hide from the truth?

"What truth?" I asked.

He came up behind me and leaned over my shoulder while I put the glasses on the tray.

"The truth lives at 1019 New Circle Road, Lot 6, a trailer camp," he said.

I looked at him and went to the refrigerator for the chilled wine and put it on the tray.

"And what name does the truth go by?" I asked.

"Avrahm Corey, Joe's father," Steven said.

He started back into the living room.

"You will stay for wine?" I asked.

He said he didn't think so.

When I got to the trailer camp, there was no one in the central office. After a while I found the small light-blue trailer Steven had told me about. I knocked on the door and a medium-sized man, about sixty, in a short gray coat, and considerable grayness in his hair and mustache, invited me in. He said he was glad to see me. He said he had been expecting me.

You're not afraid of me?" he asked, as I went inside. I had hesitated upon entering, because it had slightly alarmed me that he had known I was coming. I even resented Steven a little for telling him.

He took my coat and told me to make myself comfortable. The living room was dark with heavy purple curtains at the windows, the kind one sees at confessional boxes; the rug and the sofa were the same wine-like hue. He told me to sit down. It was one of those sturdy, old-fashioned sofas, the kind that last for years and that you pass on to your children. There were carved wooden armrests. In fact, the whole room was rich greens and wines. It was a small, close room but not stuffy. There was an antique mirror over an artificial mantelpiece.

He had the tea hot and waiting beside a tray of cookies on the coffee table. He said he hoped I liked tea. I said I did. He said not many people like tea.

"Joey didn't say anything about a wedding," he said. "I hope you like the house."

"It's perfect," I said. "But why did you move away if you didn't know he was married?"

"I haven't lived there for years," he said. "I never liked it there."

He offered me cookies. "Now help yourself. Don't be afraid. Don't be afraid of me."

I said I wasn't afraid. I took a cookie and sat back.

"I was a sea captain in the Navy," he said. "When Joe was a boy he was a lean sickly lad with a lewd mother. I divorced her and took the boy with me. Now she is leading a wicked life in Winchester. His childhood is lost and dead. I tried to save him from this memory."

He was acting as strangely as Joseph. He cried out, "I won't go near him!" Then he was calm, almost as if the scream had not happened. "Now come meet Charles, then you'll go home so your husband will not feel your absence." He sounded tired and sad at the end.

Charles was a short, thin, almost emaciated man of about Joseph's father's age. His hair was very gray and he wore it in a bush. His clothes were less elegant than Avrahm's. He wore khaki trousers and a light-blue shirt opened at the collar. He held out a warm hand and said he was glad to meet me. He said he was Joseph's uncle. Then Uncle Charles and Joseph's father said goodbye, and Joseph's father said I was never to come again.

I rode home in a taxi. The way the man had spoken, his deliberate incoherency, had given me a strange feeling. For I was certain it was deliberate. It had to be.

When I got home, Joseph was sitting on a hassock by the window. He was reading something. He looked up when I came in and I expected him to ask where I had been, but he didn't.

"I've been looking at this map of Japan," he said. "All the strange names and places. It makes one feel so very happy."

"I suppose so," I said.

He put the map down.

"Was it a nice tea party?" he asked.

"What do you mean?"

"With Father," he said. He looked at me hard.

"We had tea," I said. I tried to return the hard look. I wanted to know how he found out.

"Steven told you where to find him, didn't he?" Joseph asked. He sounded angry, but he wasn't upset at all. He looked back down at his Japanese map. "It makes one feel so very happy," he repeated.

He looked up at me again. "Tomorrow I'll go see him. Was Charlie Steele there?"

"Your uncle?"

"He's not my uncle. His name's Charlie Steele. He's my father's friend. They were at sea together. Now they're on land."

"Tomorrow I'll go see them," he said.

It disturbed me but I didn't say anything.

Joseph went and returned, but nothing happened. I didn't really know what was supposed to happen, only that I had dreaded his going and even more his returning afterwards.

"He looks well," Joseph said. "You know, I haven't seen him in years."

"I'm glad you're glad you went," I said.

"I didn't say I was glad I went." He sat down on the couch.

That night Steven came, and he and Joseph said scarcely a word to each other. I went out into the kitchen to get something, and when I came back I heard Steven saying, "Anything can happen when you're straddling three cultures—Western, Oriental, and our own, or the one we're trying to define for ourselves."

Joseph merely grunted an affirmative, and the conversation ended.

Steven said he had better be going.

"Stay, Steven," I said.

"I thought of telephoning," he said. "I just wanted to know how you were."

"I'm glad you came," I said.

Steven went out the door.

The rain falling hard made Joseph turn to the window.

"Steven'll get caught in it," he said. He turned off the light.

"Good night, Dora," he said.

I almost didn't say, "Good night, Joe."

For the next few weeks there was some kind of enmity between Joseph and Steven. I heard from Steven more often now, but less in person. He would drop notes, send fragmented telegrams. Once he even sent a piece of the beard he was growing. "I smoke cigarette after cigarette and read detective stories," he told me. Why detective stories, I wondered. Steven worried me. He was still at the university, and that pleased me very much. Although he was this sort of communication fanatic, somehow I still felt he could handle himself and his life.

I didn't know the same of myself now. Joseph went on with his life of rituals and tranquilizers. Then I got the note from Steven that said, "You must do it, you have to." I knew what he wanted. I went to see him.

Steven had a full beard and he looked like a prophet in his attic apartment. He said he would shave it off soon. He said the reason for it was no longer there.

We sat down at a square, rough-hewn wooden table and drank coffee and talked for a while, small talk, then, "Steven, you said I had to do it. Why?"

"He has to go back," Steven said.

"He's done nothing, Steven. He's been good, very good."

"Someone broke into the storage building at Greenwood Cemetery and took the riding mower and rode it all over the grounds."

"He went out last night, for a walk, he said. How do you know he did it?"

"I was there. He came and got me and took me there."

"Why there?"

"He says his mother lives there. She went crazy in that house. That's why Avrahm moved away. That's why he never liked it there."

"You don't believe that," I said.

He said he didn't know. I looked at him.

"He never lived with her more than two years, his father took him away," he said.

"He's not mad, Steven," I said. "Last night when we were together, he said 'You love me, Dora, I know you love me.' He's not mad. I can't send him away. Love can save. I know it can."

"What if he goes away?"

"I want to go home, Steven. Will you take me?"

He said he would.

When we got home, Joseph was gone.

I looked at Steven. "You knew," I said. "How did you know?"

He said he hadn't known. He said it was no use trying to get him to come back. He would come back if he wanted to, and if he didn't, well, he wouldn't. I said I hoped he was safe.

"Anything could happen to a madman, running about without any clothes on," Steven said. "I mean, in the ihram."

"You're cruel, Steven," I said. "You were cruel to drive him away."

"He wanted to go," Steven said. "He wanted to break away from everything, everyone. I only helped him along. All his life he's been running away from things, but for running he was always returning to them. To Greenwood, to his father's trailer, to the house. Even marriage was no way out. He wanted to be a priest, you know, but he didn't like the idea of having to take confessions."

I thought of the purple confessional curtains in his father's trailer.

"I know where he is," I said.

When Steven and I arrived at the trailer, it was ten o'clock at night, and Charles was sitting in a lawn chair outside the door.

"Why are you out here, Mr. Steele?" I asked.

He looked at me.

"You called me Mister," he said. "You think I'm an old man. I'm not an old man, I'm an old woman. My name's Charlene Steele. I'm not an old man, I'm an old woman. You thought I was an old man. I was born sixty-eight years ago. One of the Knox County Steeles. Charlene."

Steven was standing away from us. I went over to him.

"Are you in on this too?" I asked, bitterly.

Steven didn't say anything. He was listening for something.

"What is it?" I asked.

"I thought I heard the credo," he said.

"The Creed?"

"*I believe in the Almighty Father, Creator of Heaven and Earth . . . resurrection of the flesh and life eternal. . . . Pray for us sinners now and at the hour . . .*" It was Joseph's voice.

I followed Steven inside. When we got there Joseph was not there. Only Avrahm was sitting in the big purple chair, looking at us vaguely.

"He climbed out the window," he said. "He stole my gun and climbed out the window."

"I'm frightened," I said.

"He never liked the Mass," Avrahm said.

Steven and I started out the door.

"He said he was going back to the house," Avrahm called.

We found Joseph in the house, decked in priest's robes.

"Where have you been?" Steven asked.

"With Brahman."

"You have your facts wrong," Steven said. "You cannot be with Brahman. You have to become Brahman."

"Then I have become Brahman," Joseph said.

Steven and I must have seen the gun hidden under the skirt of his cassock at the same time, for I started to say something, but Steven quieted me with a wave of his hand. We stood there, watching Joseph.

"Your father says somebody stole his gun," Steven said. "He's an old man and I don't think he knows what happened to his gun and has forgotten what he did with it."

"He gave it to me," Joseph said.

"The way he gave it to your mother," Steven said.

Joseph shook his head fervently. Up till then he had sat calmly, holding his gun under his skirts.

"He won't," he shouted. He ran to the door.

"He's gone," Steven said. "He took the trailer and left."

"I'll find him."

"It's dark out," Steven said.

Joseph was going out the door. I wanted to stop him or go with him, but Steven pushed me gently aside.

"Do you like it here?" he asked quickly.

"Yes, they give me my meals but I can't pray. This is a nice place. I have a bad head you know. Been here two years, they put things on my head. My wife is in the country. She has a brother. I have a very bad head you know." He had come away from the door. He was not talking to Steven.

Steven grabbed a Kafka book from the shelf.

"Do you want this book?"

"No. I have a bad head." He was fingering his forehead now, and he sat down on the floor, his legs folded under him, hidden under his skirts. The gun was in his lap.

"They are learning me to read again," he said simply. "The head people. He loaned me the gun." He rose up again, not excited. "Yes I like it here," he said. Then he said suddenly, "I'm tired, Dora. Very tired, Dora. Tomorrow—I'll find him."

Steven took the gun and I took Joseph by the arm.

When I came downstairs, Steven was standing in the living room.

"Is it true about his mother?" I asked.

"Only partly. Only there was a different kind of weapon. He left her alone in the house. He called it working out her own salvation. He left her and took the boy."

"I'll never leave Joseph," I said.

"He was always afraid he'd become like his father," Steven said.

"I thought it was his mother who was insane."

Steven nodded. "He went away to live in his trailer. He left her here in the house. It was the loneliness, the house that drove her mad. She began walking the streets. Avrahm's always blamed her for that. A way of absolving himself. I think Joseph went there tonight to put the blame where it belongs. To take his father's confession. I don't think the old man could stand it very well."

"Will Joseph leave?"

"Joseph won't go, ever, unless you send him away."

"Why the priest outfit?" I asked.

"Confession-absolution. The whole guilt ritual. Schizophrenia. Self-guilt too. He's assuming two roles. Do you know anything about shamanism?"

"Yes. The shaman—priest figure, magician, curer, saint."

"He's made himself both the doctor and the patient, the curer and the ill. He has made himself the priest figure, working his own magic."

"Working his own salvation," I said. "But can he be . . . saved?"

"I don't know," Steven said. "One never knows."

"One knows, yes. One always knows," I said.

Steven said he had spent a long time trying to protect me from Joseph, now he said I could find my own way. When he started to go, I took him by the arm.

"Steven, do you believe everything you've told me?" I asked.

He looked hostile, impenetrable, as if he were shielding himself from something, or someone, then he broke into an uneven, vague half-smile.

"I was protecting myself, too," he said.

At first I didn't know what he meant.

I started to go with him to the door, but he said he could find his way out.

I went upstairs and found Joseph, asleep.

THE ROUNDHOUSE

I DIDN'T KNOW what was wrong with him, even after I went to see him. I'd heard at work that he was sick, and asked if he had anybody to do for him. They said he had a room in Will Darcy's rooming house. He didn't have a family, and nobody knew anything about him, and there was no one to take care of him. I hadn't known him long, just three weeks, and we'd never really said more than "Hi." He was a quiet man. He was the kind you feel close to even though you've said no more than "Hi."

I was working at the roundhouse in Garrett, Indiana. Garrett, not Gary. Just after the war, the first one. The roundhouse was where the trains came in. It was our job to polish the parts, and keep the engines shining. I was hired during the war, when they were hiring women. I'd been working a year there, and my kids were going to school, when he came. He never said anything to anybody. He did his work. He did more work than he had to, and he didn't talk to anyone. He looked like a foreigner, reddish brown. Maybe he was a Negro, maybe he was Puerto Rican or something or maybe mixed. People said maybe he couldn't speak English. He never bothered anybody, and nobody bothered him. He came to work and he left work and he never talked. I don't even know if he stopped for lunch.

One day we'd been assigned to the same engine. He was there before I was, polishing away. He looked up when I came. "Hi," I said. He didn't smile. He looked back down. He wasn't being unfriendly. There are some people who just don't talk. I could tell he knew English though. I don't know how but I could tell. He didn't have the look of someone who didn't know the language.

We worked. At lunchtime I quit and started away but saw he was still working. I started to ask, "Aren't you going to have lunch?" but didn't. I thought maybe he wouldn't want me to.

I went and sat down on a bench, eating a sandwich. Some other people were there. Joe McDowell was there.

"Did he say anything to you?" he asked.

"He said 'Hi,'" I said.

"That's more than he said to me," McDowell said. "I worked with him a whole day. Funny thing, though. I didn't feel uncomfortable. Most people don't talk, you feel uncomfortable as hell. With him you don't."

"I know," I said. "It's nice."

"Nobody knows anything about him," McDowell said. "Henderson says he's taken a room over at Darcy's place. That's not far from where you live. I've heard of people that don't talk much. He don't talk at all."

"He probably does when he has to," I said.

"Ask for a job or a room," McDowell said, not sarcastically.

"Anyway, he seems very nice," I said.

McDowell nodded. It was time to start working again. Four more hours. The kids would be home from school.

When five o'clock came, he stopped work and left. He was practically the first to be gone. It was summer and he didn't need to grab a coat. He rolled down his shirtsleeves. Neither Darcy's nor where I lived was far from the station, so we both walked home, about a fifteen or twenty minute walk, a half hour on bad days.

He walked fast. I didn't try to catch up with him. When I got to the street, he was a block ahead of me. I saw him turn into the rooming house. I passed where he lived and walked a block more up the street.

The next day we walked home the same way, he walking rapidly ahead again. He seemed always in a hurry, even when he worked. He worked hard and fast. It was a wonder the men hadn't got together and told him to slow down, he made the others look bad, but people liked him, though he didn't talk much. As I said, he was walking ahead and turned in at his gate, but when I passed the rooming house this time, he had not gone in the door, but was standing there, his hand on the doorknob, his head turned looking at me. He didn't say anything and went inside. I walked on. I felt funny.

"I knew a switchman I worked with," McDowell was saying, then he stopped and looked up.

I looked up. *He* was standing there, looking down at me.

"I want to walk you home," he said to me.

"O-kay," I said, bewildered. Then he walked away. McDowell looked at me and grinned.

When I got outside, he was waiting for me. It had been cooler this morning and he had a jacket slung over his shoulder. He looked down and smiled. We started walking.

"How are you?" I asked.

"Okay," he said.

We walked on.

"I didn't know you came this way," he said, the first time he'd said more than a word or two. "We could have walked together before."

Now I didn't say anything.

"You live a block away from me," he said. I wondered how he knew. "In a house."

"I have two kids," I said.

"You're married?" he asked, as if I might not be.

"I was."

"How do you mean?"

"He died."

"In the war?"

"No."

I was waiting for him to ask how, like most people had, but he didn't. He seemed to feel if I wanted him to know I'd tell him. I wanted him to know. "From alcohol," I said.

"Oh," he said. I guess I hadn't really expected an "I'm sorry" from him either. The platitudes. I guess he didn't do things that way.

Then we were at the boarding house. I was stopping for him to turn in, but he didn't. He took my elbow slightly.

"I'll see you home," he said.

He saw me home, and then went back. I went inside.

"Who's he?" Jean asked. "He's handsome." Jean was my daughter, thirteen, with her hairs in plaits.

"His name's . . . I don't know his name. He works where I work."

"I haven't seen him before."

"He hasn't walked me home before. Where's Ben?"

"He's in the kitchen."

Ben was my son. He was fourteen. He was light, almost white. Jean was brown. My grandmother had been white. It was hard explaining to people. It was better in Indiana.

"How was school?" I asked.

"The same."

"Much homework?"

"Yes."

Ben came in and said, "Hi." I started supper.

"Mama's got a beau," I heard Jean tell Ben.

"I have not," I called. "He works at the roundhouse."

"He walked her home," Jean said, triumphantly. "He's good-looking," she added. "You'll have to check him out."

I didn't hear Ben say anything. I was thinking Ben might like him.

The next day I didn't see him at all, not even after work, and the day after he was not there. I had lunch with McDowell.

"He's probably gone," McDowell said.

"Gone?" I asked.

"You know how it is with them. Come to one town. Hold down a job for a while. Have to keep moving."

"You don't mean he's running from the law?"

"Don't have to be the law."

"What then?"

"Himself. Somebody. How should I know?"

"I didn't know his name," I said.

"James Buchanan Jones, named for the president. Henderson says he calls himself Jake. Wants the people that know him to."

Lunchtime was over. I went back to work.

The next day, McDowell came over to where I was working.

"Henderson says Jake's sick."

"What's wrong?"

"Don't know."

"Hasn't anybody been to see about him?"

"Don't think so. He didn't get close with people."

I frowned and put down the rag and started away. McDowell grabbed my arm.

"Where *you* going?" he asked.

"To see about him."

"The Man won't like it, stopping on the job."

"I don't care."

"You've got two kids."

"Tell him I got sick, Joe."

Joe shook his head slowly.

"It's an hour till lunch," he said.

"All right." I picked up the rag.

He started away.

"Thanks, Joe," I called. He nodded.

At lunchtime I went outside.

"What did the boss say when I didn't come back?" I asked McDowell, the first thing in the morning, before I even started.

"I told him you got sick," he said.

"Thank you."

"How is he?"

"Fever. Wouldn't let me call a doctor. I'm doing what I can. He didn't have any food."

"How are you going to work and take care of him and yourself and the kids?"

"I can manage," I said.

"If you need me you know where to reach me," he said.

"Sure, Joe," I said. I thanked him again. He tapped my arm and went to work. I thought I wouldn't know what to do without him. He had been awfully good to me and the kids.

That afternoon I stopped at the rooming house before going home. I had a bundle with me. A loaf of bread and some curtains. I put the bundle down and went over to him and placed my hand on his forehead. He hadn't been able to shave for about a week now.

"How do you feel?" I asked.

"Better, thanks to you," he said.

"You still have a fever," I said.

I went over to the bundle and started taking the curtains out.

"What are they for? I have curtains," he said.

"Your curtains are ugly," I said.

"They're not, if you don't look at them," he said.

"These you can look at," I said, and started putting the curtains up. The window was small and faced the street. There was only the bed in the room and a chest of drawers, a table and chair.

"Now you won't be able to tell I'm a bachelor," he said.

"I can tell," I said.

I sat down in the chair.

"I've got to go home and fix supper," I said. "I'll be back a little later and bring you something over."

I started up to go but he took one of my hands in both his and said thank you. I smiled and went home.

I went back with some chicken soup. He didn't eat much.

"Your fever's going down," I said. "You couldn't tell by the way you eat, though."

"I never eat much. You have to learn not to."

"Joe McDowell says you're the kind of person that never stays in one place."

"I guess that's right," he said.

"Where are you from?" I asked.

He didn't answer. I didn't press him to.

"You have kids," he said. "What are they like?"

"They're nice," I said.

"You know you live with people a long time and then when somebody asks you what they're like you say they're nice. I guess that's all you can say really." He wasn't being sarcastic.

"I have their pictures," I said. I took out a billfold from my purse and opened it and showed him their pictures.

"The boy's half white," he said.

"Is there a crime against having white blood?" I asked. I was jumpy on that subject.

"The same crime as having black," he said.

"My grandmother," I said.

"You don't have to explain," he said.

"I know," I said.

"They say my mother was a gypsy," he said. "If she showed anybody my picture they would have asked, 'What makes the boy so brown?'"

"You didn't know her?"

"I didn't know her or my father," he said. "I grew up in homes."

"I'm sorry."

He grew angry suddenly. "Don't say you're sorry."

"Okay, Jake." I was hurt.

He touched my hand.

"Don't take it wrong," he said.

"Okay."

I stood up, "I'd better go."

"You're not angry?"

"No, no."

"Promise?"

"I promise."

The next day I saw McDowell for lunch.

"How's he doing?" he asked.

"The fever's almost gone," I said. "I think it's just overwork. He doesn't take care of himself. He doesn't eat."

"He needs a wife," Joe said.

I didn't say anything.

In a couple of days, Jake was well but didn't come back to work again. He had done what McDowell said people like that did.

"You miss him don't you?" McDowell said. "You knew what he'd do. Men like that . . ."

"Yeah, I know about men like that," I said.

He touched my arm. "I'm sorry," he said.

"Don't be," I said.

When the war was over and the men had come home, the roundhouse had kept some of us on, mostly those who didn't have husbands. Now they were laying some of us off again or reducing our hours. My hours had been reduced, and what I was making now would hardly buy chicken feed, less more support two kids.

When somebody started paying my grocery bills and coal bills, the first person I thought of was McDowell.

"What are you doing?" I asked Joe. I explained. He said he wasn't doing anything. No, it couldn't be, I decided.

The mysterious bill payments went on for several months. I asked the store not to take any more money, but they said there was nothing they could do about it.

I was in the kitchen fixing supper when the doorbell rang. Jean went to answer it. She came back into the kitchen, smiling.

"Who is it?" I asked.

"Go see," she said.

I frowned and wiped my hands on my apron. I stopped in the doorway to the hall.

"Jake!" I exclaimed. I went over to him. "How are you?"

"Very well," he said. "You look well."

There was a bench in the hall.

"Let's sit down," I said.

He said he'd rather stand, and if things went well then we could sit down. I asked him what he was talking about.

He said he wanted to take care of me. He said I had taken care of him when he was sick, and now he was ready to take care of me.

I looked up at him. He wasn't smiling. He was waiting.

I sat down.

He sat down beside me.

LEGEND

THE BRIDGE HAS THE SMELL OF A MAN. There are too many bumps in the bridge, too many groans. People who know the legend of Eph Grizzard hold their breath when they go over. White people, sometimes black, hold their breath when they go over. In all these years, the bridge has not collapsed. Men are afraid to tear it down. They are afraid to keep it up. They built another bridge beside it.

Eph Grizzard? His body hangs under the bridge. They say he raped a white woman. A mob brought him there and hanged him. Her father came and got him.

Come on, Eph.

He locked him in her room and said, *Now take her*, while he watched and watched and watched.

Satisfied? The father. Some say the old man was crazy. He came and got his blackest buck.

Niggers caint love, he said. *I'll watch and see.*

Some said the old man was crazy. Eph, black-skinned, the richest black. Some say the old man was drunk, he'd had a bottle, he grinned when his daughter screamed.

Here, take her. Here, Eph. Here, Eph. Here, Eph.

Some say when you pass the bridge it has the smell of a man. The wind in the hemp. Some say when the moon is ripe you can see his body hanging. Just barely. That his body spills over in the river like whiskey from a bottle. But they say nobody cut the rope. Nobody *dared* cut the rope. Nobody ever cut Eph Grizzard's body down. The rope swung in the wind till time took care of him.

It's true, sho nuff, it's true, you hear the black folks say. People even scared to whistle old Eph Grizzard's name.

It's true, sho nuff, it's true.

Some say Eph Grizzard got away to Kansas. Nobody ever looked to see his body. Scared to look.

Wall, they marched ole Eph up Firs Avenue then tied the rope and throwed him over he hanged there from three o'clock to six o'clock they's scared to cut him down.

How he get down?

Nobody know.

Wind through hemp. Hear, Eph. A black-skin nigger, they say his tribe were wealthy juju men and women.

Eph Grizzard sees you, the children say.

Yeah, the girl went crazy. She bore a nigger son.

Where is he?

No, nobody know. So long ago. Some say she kilt it.

Eph Grizzard sees you, his head hung low.

They say his father was a juju man. They scared to cut him down.

Jesus will come and cut him down, an old woman says.

Time and the wind took care of him. Time and the river. Do you see his eyes? His head hung low.

His soul'll be a tongue when he reach the Lord Jesus, an old woman says. *He'll tell it all.*

The wind in the copper trees.

Can't you hear Eph Grizzard?

The white man made me take her so he could watch, a shotgun at my back. The old man mumbling, *Niggers caint.*

The wind wrings the water. Boards on the bridge black as shade.

Here, take her, you black blood nigger. Fuck for Christ's sake.

The girl went crazy.

The Son of God was never born to no white woman, not even once.

The girl went crazy giving birth, her father watching, fists clinching jaws. But Eph Grizzard has been hanging. Can you see his eyes?

The bridge collapses, caving in like the buttocks of a woman. Hemp in the wind. His body dropped to water long ago. *No one trode over me.* They all were scared to take him down. Here, take him down. His soul is a tongue that can't keep quiet.

Her father gave that ole white girl to me hisself.

A QUIET PLACE FOR THE SUMMER

SHE WAS LIVING IN VERMONT and renting a country house from one of her professors. He had advertised for someone to live in and take care of the place. Someone quiet who wouldn't "throw parties." She had told him that she was looking for a quiet place for the summer.

"I thought about asking you," he said. "But I thought perhaps you'd want to spend the summer in Georgia."

"No."

"I'd like you to stay here. I'd like a friend."

She stood saying nothing, surprised and glad he'd called her that.

When she came to get the key, he opened the door. He was wearing jeans and a thin gray sweater. She had never seen him out of the suit and tie, and really didn't think of him wearing anything else. He took her bag and put it down in the corner near the writing desk.

"Here are the keys," he said. "I should be back by the time the dorms open. If not, you can leave them with the department secretary."

"Okay," she said. She stood there feeling awkward in his house.

He stood with his hands in his pockets.

"You haven't seen the house," he said. "That's the study."

She followed him into a room off from the living room.

"Do you collect antiques?" she asked.

"Not really. This just isn't the kind of house for modern furniture," he said.

She nodded, looking at the old furniture, standing next to a framed letter on the wall.

"One of my forefathers," he said. "From the nineteenth century."

She looked at it a moment, stared down at the wood floor. He took her arm lightly and they went through the rest of the house, coming back to the living room.

"Well, I hope you like staying here," he said.

He seemed more nervous and on edge in his own house. When she'd come to the office he was comfortable and sure and self-contained.

She looked at a picture of a white man and woman on the wall. They both stood stiffly. The man held his hand inside his coat, like Napoleon. They are probably his ancestors, she thought.

"That's my great-grandmother and great-grandfather," he said looking at her face. "They must be nervous. When I get nervous I stiffen up."

She smiled. It was as if he read her thoughts. It made her feel happy. They stood for a moment saying nothing. Then he said he had to go. She sighed. She hadn't meant to. She felt embarrassed.

"I hope you get some good work done," he said, as if he hadn't heard.

He patted her shoulder. He turned away from her slightly. She watched the side of his face, his hair worn like the man in the picture. He turned to her.

"Well, take care. Have a good summer."

"You too."

"I'll see you in class next fall."

"Okay."

She wanted to say more but didn't know what. He went out the door. He looked like he was walking sideways. He waved to her. She smiled. She watched him and then she turned to watch the man who held his hand inside his coat.

Coleman was the man who took care of the trees. He said trees were like children, that if you took care of them they would grow right. She had told him that her favorite was the tree that was thick-limbed and crooked, the one that had a hole in its center.

"Yes, this is a beautiful tree," he had said. "Some people would look at her and think she was deformed, but she's not. She is very beautiful. You like her because when you look at her it's like looking into a cave."

She didn't answer. He went on talking.

"I like her because I replanted her here. I saw her in the woods and I said I must have her and so I replanted her here. And I've taken care of her and she's still here. She's my friend." He smiled. "In the spring, when the sap runs, that's the best time. You gather it in buckets. A spoon of milk keeps it from boiling over. A tree can be so still and have so much going on inside of it. There are people like that, you know."

She said, "Yes." Then she said, "I like to look at the trees in winter."

"Nothing happens then."

"I like to see them standing there. They must be still alive."

"They live. They wait to be reborn," he said and then he went down to the small trees in the nursery. She watched him walk, the bow in his slender legs.

"What is it?" Calvin asked.

"Nothing."

He was silent, then he had told her, "You like him because he's here. If he were anyone else and here you would still think you were . . ."

"No."

"You like him?"

"Yes. Don't you?"

He shrugged, then asked, "When do you go out there?"

"Next week."

"He won't be there, will he?"

"No, of course not."

He said nothing. She was standing with him at the train station. He ran his hand along the side of her neck.

"You don't think I should trust him?" she asked.

"I didn't say that."

"What then?"

"Give me a kiss," he said suddenly.

She'd started to kiss him on the side of the face, but he kissed her mouth.

"Don't think of you and him."

"What?"

"Just don't think there's anything. He's probably not a bad dude. But you don't know these people."

"I . . ."

He got on the train without turning his head.

"You must have many voices in you," she said to the tree.

Coleman whispered behind her, "Yes."

She jumped, she turned around and smiled. She ran her long fingers through her short hair, looking at him quizzically.

"She knows that words must be used with care."

She smiled.

"Are you the girl from the college Professor Martin said would be staying here?"

"Yes. Who are you?"

"My name's Coleman. I take care of the grounds. The trees mostly. I live down the road a piece. . . . He said you'd be writing stories."

"Yes," she said, embarrassed.

Saying nothing, he put his hand through the cave in the tree.

"I was in a little town in France," Coleman said.

She had brought tea out onto the porch and they were sitting, talking.

"We weren't supposed to shoot sparrows," he said. "We'd ride through the next town so we could say we'd shot them passing through. The thing was small and brown and delicious and I ate it only because everybody else did."

He stopped. She wondered if he had finished the story. She did not know what the point of it was.

He asked, "What are you and Professor Martin?"

"What do you mean?"

"What are you to each other?"

"Friends."

"That's all?"

"Yes."

He said nothing. Then he laughed. She pushed her feet up under her. She was wearing a long house dress. She covered her knees.

"You know a lot of people around here?" she asked. "Oh, you must."

He smiled. "No. I know a few people, but I know them well. That's better than knowing a lot of people just a little, don't you think?"

She nodded. He straightened his legs out and looked at his shoes.

"These shoes were made for the desert. I wore them here and walked out in the wet grass and they came to pieces. They're handmade. I can't remember what kind of coin I bought them with."

She looked at him.

"I didn't buy them here, I mean. I didn't buy them in this country."

She felt she should ask him where he got them, but didn't. A cat passed by on the grass and stood rubbing her fur against one of the trees. She watched.

"I tried to clip her this morning," he said. "She wouldn't let me."

"Clip her?"

"Her claws are too long. If you clip them too far, they will bleed."

"Oh . . . have you clipped her before?"

"Yeah. She'll come when she's a mind to. . . . Have you met his wife?"

She looked up at him and then stared down at her hands.

"Not many people know," he said. "She goes away for years at a time and then when she returns he takes her back and they are very happy."

"I believe you're lying."

He nodded, resting his chin on his chest.

"Isn't that a story for you?" he asked, laughing.

She turned away from him, looking out at the trees.

"Where you from?" he asked, raising his head.

"Georgia."

"You don't talk like it."

"Well, uh, I've been here for five years."

"You go home sometimes, don't you?"

"Yeah. This is the first vacation I haven't."

"You don't have to lose your accent."

"No, I guess not."

"No, you don't. Not unless you want to."

She said nothing, then she asked, "Are you from here?"

"Yeah, I'm an old Vermont man. We go back for generations. I've been a lot of places, though. I was a sailor, I was in the Merchant Marine. I've done some logging. I owned a little store over in Quaker country. Then I came back. And I still got my accent. Though I've got many voices."

She smiled, looking at the lines in his forehead.

"Last time it was with a young boy," he said.

"What?"

"She went away with. Called himself a poet. One of the professor's students."

"Oh."

"What happened was she went and sat in on one of his classes and took to one of the boys. A bright kid. Said all he wanted to do was write poetry, though. Said his father didn't understand. Wanted him to be a pharmacist. She went off with him the next day. Or took him with her. . . . Does this story scare you?"

"What?"

"About the woman. That some night you'll be sleeping and a strange woman will come into the house and find you in her bed."

She didn't answer, then she shook her head.

"Don't nobody know about it but me and you."

"And him."

"Yeah. Do you think he's handsome?"

"I guess."

"Yeah, some women think he is handsome."

"We don't know each other very well."

"Why did you pretend to?"

"I didn't pretend to."

"You wanted me to think so."

"No."

He stared at her.

"Have you ever seen the woman?" she asked suddenly.

He leaned back in his chair and laughed.

"Aren't you going to speak?"

She turned her head. It was Calvin. He took her arm and they went together to the cafeteria for brunch. Cream cheese, toast, sausage, eggs. It was Sunday.

"Have you been reading any Eliot lately?" he asked.

She shook her head.

She'd read him T. S. Eliot the first time they'd spent together. He'd listened but afterwards laughed at her, and every time he'd seen her he'd ask about Eliot. He'd said Eliot had no real feeling.

"You're more interesting than that," he'd said. "Or you could be."

He'd touched the corners of her eyes.

"There's Professor Martin," he whispered.

He watched her eyes brighten, then when she saw there was no one, they darkened, she stared down at her plate.

"Once I went in and she was sitting in the living room at that table, the one under the picture of Napoleon. Just sitting there. She had a cup of coffee and her hair was wet and stringy. I have a key to the house and sometimes I bring kindling in—that's what I was doing—I had an armload of kindling. She looked up, smiled, and just sat there. I didn't say anything to her. I just went over to the fireplace and put the kindling down.

"'I feel I must be crazy.'

"I wasn't sure I heard her. 'What?'

"'I feel I must be crazy.'

"She's a good-looking woman, you know. She's as old as the professor—has gray in her hair and lines around her eyes and everything. But you know how some women stay good-looking. It's the bone structure. She's real quiet most of the time. She's only been here a few times since I worked here. A real mystery. And most of the time she never said a thing to me even when I seen her. That's why I didn't speak. But this time I was standing there and she had turned her head and was looking at me. She had some pictures spread out.

"'Come and look at my pictures.'

"I went over but what I wanted to do was just get out of there. Professor Martin might come anytime. She made me nervous. You'd look at her you wouldn't think she was a dangerous woman—all thin and sandy-haired—except maybe to *him* but she still made me nervous. I went over to the table though and stood, kind of away from her.

"'Sit down.'

"I sat down.

"She spread the pictures out. They were pictures of Mexico, Latin America, like that was where she was going to go next, or where she'd been. I just sat looking at them. I was still nervous. He might come in any minute, I was thinking. Her fingernails were bit all the way down to the quick. Her fingers were nice and long though and she kept spreading the pictures in front of me. I looked up at her face real quick because I'd never seen her up close. I thought she'd be looking at the pictures. But she was looking at me. This real *strange* look on her face—don't ask me to describe it, like she was asking me a question—pushing her hair back from her face. I just sat there looking at her. Something made me feel like she was going to ask me to go somewhere with her or take her somewhere. It was just all in my mind, I knew. But I felt the moment she opened her mouth she was going to say that.

"'What's wrong?'

"'What?'

"'What's wrong with you?'

"I finally said, 'Nothing.' Then I stood up without excusing myself. I didn't excuse myself from the table or say goodbye to her. I just stood up from the table and left."

"Is that all? She didn't say anything else?"

"Naw. That's strange, ain't it?"

"Yes."

"I've never seen any other woman in this house," he said. "Not before you."

"Hasn't he . . . been with other women? . . . You said she goes away so many years at a time."

"I reckon he's *been* with them—but not here."

She stuck her hands into the pockets of her dress, leaning forward, shaking her head.

"I'm telling you what I saw. I'm just wondering what would happen if she did come back and find you here. A pretty young girl."

"We're not lovers or anything."

"She wouldn't know that."

"You'd tell her."

"Would I? Maybe I wouldn't."

"She has other men anyway. Even if we were lovers."

"But he's never had any woman here. And she always takes her men away somewhere. . . . You wouldn't be frightened if she came?"

She shook her head, "No. I'd just explain. Why did he go away if what you say is true? That he never knows when to expect her."

"Search me."

"Maybe she wrote him a letter this time to meet her someplace," she said. "Maybe they're spending the summer together someplace. In Mexico."

He shrugged.

She closed her eyes, then she smiled suddenly, looking at him, "I remember once when I was standing outside his office. That was when I was a freshman and hardly even knew him.

"'Why do you persecute me?'

"That's what I heard him say. I was the only one standing out in the hall. I was holding my books tight against my chest. The door was closed. I was standing there for a long time. The room was real quiet. I didn't know if I should knock or what. I just stood there. And then I heard a woman's voice say real softly,

"'I'll be here this evening and then I've got to go up to Canada.'

"'You can't stay longer? You could stay a week or two. You could stay a few days.'

"'I can't.'

"Then a woman came out. She walked past me quickly. I can't remember what she looked like. I didn't know who she might have been.

"I didn't know whether to go in or not. The door was open but I stood there and then he came to the door. He saw me and jumped. He acted nervous. He said, 'Come in.' I went in and just stood there. He was supposed to talk with me about a paper but he must have forgot. He said, 'What is it? What do you want?' I told him. He said, 'Sit down' and then he started to say something about the paper. He had it out. He kept looking at it and then he said, 'I'm sorry, but I've got to meet somebody back at the house.' He got up and started out. 'Could you pull the door to.' I said, 'Yes.' He turned and looked at me and frowned and then he smiled. He oversmiled."

He laughed and clapped his hands. She touched his hair and the side of his face. She frowned and pulled her hand away. She held her hand in her lap.

"It's all right," he said.

"What?"

He didn't answer, then he said, "They stand still but everything is happening inside of them. A person shouldn't stand still. A person doesn't have to. You can let as much that's happening inside of you out—whatever you want to. I've got you talking now. You didn't say much when we first met."

"Some."

"I wonder how a tree feels when it lets go a fruit," he said.

"Some Spanish poet called them the skeletons of dead beauties," she said.

"What?"

"Trees in the winter."

He said nothing. He asked if she wanted to go to the carnival.

"Yes."

"It's here every year. I haven't been in many years."

"I haven't been to one since I was twelve."

"I don't think he even sleeps with her."

She turned her head aside and stared at the trees again.

Guns to shoot wooden ducks. A man tells their weight and how old they are. He is right. The man is drunk off beer, a bottle beside him on the ground. Still he is right. The carnival grounds are dark and they walk on small gray rocks. They stand in the lights of the merry-go-round. They go into the fun house. They sit in a small cart and he puts his arm around her. When they are outside it is raining. Coleman buys them milkshakes. She watches the rain drop in hers. They are silent. They walk around on small rocks.

"Have you ever been drunk?" he asks.

"No."

"You are afraid to."

"What?"

"You are afraid. You are afraid of real things. Sometimes it's beautiful, but other times . . . You know very little of real . . ."

She looks at him. He does not go on with what he would say. She watches the side of his face, shadows from the light and dark of the carnival, the merry-go-round, the Ferris wheel. He wants to say, "Some women have a more passionate nature than they show."

Instead he says, not looking at her, "In some cultures they don't have a word for time. I thought that everybody thought in terms of time the way we do. They don't even have a word for tomorrow. A year means nothing to them. A summer means nothing. They think in terms of eternity."

"You know so little of actual people. The world is not so vague and impersonal," Calvin had said. "Even your letters. There is no warmth. I want to feel as if I am being spoken to by a live woman."

"If I touch your leg you will think I am getting fresh with you. In some places a woman's leg means nothing. The same as if I touched the side of your face. Ah, and if I were to touch the side of your face in . . . And there are places where I could touch the tips of your breasts and you would think nothing of it. You would smile at me."

"You have no social consciousness," Calvin said.

She watched him on the rostrum standing with the tall thin girl. The one who'd cut her hair near bald. The one in her dorm who would kiss you one moment and scream at you the next. The one she feared and respected. At first Calvin had asked her to be up there with him but she'd said she couldn't. He'd looked at her a moment, then said, "No, I guess you couldn't. No, you'd be no good."

He'd turned his back on her, then he turned around and touched her arm. "Even if you don't know what to talk about, you could read something. Something about Georgia. Something about your people. Something to let us know you're with us."

She stood there. She wanted to tell him she'd be too shy, afraid the others wouldn't like it. She knew he'd take her silence wrong.

"I'd be there," he said.

She still said nothing.

"Aw, skip it," he said, turning away.

"When I was twenty I was surprised at being twenty. But now I'm no longer surprised. . . ."

"You do not realize."

"What?"

"That you're beautiful."

"What do you think of me?"

"Because they have taught you so long that you are not."

"And you teach me!"

"What are you doing here anyway?"

"What about the collective consciousness of the people? We are the people who will redeem the human race."

"Do you think you'll want to stay here?" Professor Martin asked.

"Yes. I like New England. The people aren't so . . . narrow."

He laughed, his head thrown back. "You'll learn. You're young. How old are you? Seventeen? You haven't been here long enough. You'll find . . . I have an aunt who'd . . . You'll learn."

He handed her a book by Randall Jarrell.

Calvin had his hands on her arms and held her firmly, staring into her eyes. When she didn't answer he shook his head, then pulled her closer to him and kissed her forehead and said "sweetheart" but like a friend. On the rostrum he stood with his arm around the tall girl's waist. They raised their fists. The students applauded. They kissed and raised their fists again. There was more applause. The girl beside her tapped her arm and pulled her up.

"Have you ever had something happen and it's like you've been there before or somebody says something and it's like you've heard it before? . . . Do you mind the rain?"

She looks at him. One of his eyes is red. The other is slightly brown.

"No. As long as it doesn't start pouring."

"I'll give you my cap."

"No, I'm okay."

She feels her hair tightening.

"You look like you've cut your hair."

"Oh."

She starts to put her hand to her hair, but doesn't. It is cold for summer and the wind is blowing. He steps over a log and then reaches back to take her hand to pull her over.

"I'd think nothing of it," she says.

"What?"

"Ah, yes I would," she says, staring into his eyes, and stepping over the log.

VERSION 2

BLACK PERUVIAN SAINT yes I would go into his room but he wouldn't believe me when I said I was Jesus. Like the feel of my belly band. They say I'm wrong in the head. All these things I can do. My name's Dora, she said. Dora with the glass of milk. I can metamorphosize myself into anything you want. No, I'm Joseph. Joe if you like. I don't like Kafka. He walks too fast. Won't turn myself into an ant. A plate inside my head. Do you like me? Yes I do do do. Go inside me and I'll be.

Harpsichord sounds narrow. I take her into a little room filled with sounds against walls don't bother me. This is what I'm making. Steven, I like your sister. Made it up out of a ritual. Stop and put my hands in the air. Want her hands on my back. Dora will you marry me? Yes I will. It's so quiet here. Go out in the street alone. Sit down in a chair with a peanut butter sandwich. I'm all wrong in my head. Pull out a chair for me.

We are still all friends, aren't we? Nothing to worry about I'll make you little tea and crackles. No cheese sandwiches and bread and cheese and wine pour it in your glasses. It's all right. Why you looking at me like that? Nothing wrong with me. Put it inside of your belly.

Make my head a restricted area so bad in there bother me somebody come in my room and don't say it put it inside my eyes. I been to the Mediterranean.

I live downtown. A little dirty place in the back of a hallway. Come see me. You can wrap yourself up in my brown blanket if it's too cold. I'll wrap myself up in it too. I cut little pictures out of magazines and put them on my walls.

Some cheese have some cheese. I have little olives and cucumbers. This is my room. Come sit by the window. There's a couch there and some bread. It ain't bad in here. What do you want? My hands folded. Very glad you came.

Swallow it all down in my glass rush down in my belly. Swallow it all down in my belly till I empty it out. What do you think of me? Stick an olive in my mouth. Squirt the juice on my tongue. Make you a sandwich. Here, eat some of my sandwich. I'll walk down the stairs with you and show you how to get out of here. Is anybody watching me? Why don't you have some wine?

Watching me watching where I'm coming and going. Who are you to make me not understand? I'm here to save the world too, my slender legs folded under me. Come and go too. Don't be angry. Are you very angry? Then I'll run away from you. Don't worry me. I'm already depressed.

The night is inside fingering me like a chord. Where are you Dora? Yes down there. I been in jail then they thought I was on drugs but I said I wouldn't be on drugs because my daddy was an alcoholic. Nobody came to bail me out. Go out on bail. And my mama was a. Hold you in both of my arms till I hurt you.

Laugh and kiss your neck in a new ritual of marriage. Fingers down your back.

Tranquilize my eyes. More than your hands on my loins and forehead. Go away if you can't do it. Bricks on the floor. Purge your belly by eating nothing. Knock my door down. Save me with your kisses. See myself embarrassed by your fingers. Milk on a chair. I won't sit down on it. Fold yourself into me. I'll have more than milk. Kiss me, my eyes, my forehead, every place you can. Enfold me, put more than your arms around me. I lie on my back and sleep, your eyes in my belly. What are you, a man or a woman? I stroke your back and sleep.

Symptoms in my hair. What have I got that makes me so angry, then sad. So angry then sad. I can't say I love you just now. Love in my belly. It laps like a tongue. Let's talk as much as we can. Climb over me. Sleep with your head on my chest.

An incoherent letter from me. I am doing angry. What did they tell you? Why? Because. No, I won't tell you that.

My breath comes hard even with tranquilizers in my belly. No, I won't tell you that. I won't bother you even with my eyes. It's all in my mind. Don't take me away. Put an overcoat over me in the cold.

They think I'm on drugs or something. I wouldn't do that. My daddy's an alcoholic. Got me sitting in this chair. Put my feet up in this chair. Why did you bring me here? Because I. Feet caked with dirt. Don't look at me. Do I know you? I don't know you. This is all in my eyes. I don't even know you. Come back here with me. Dora called you didn't she? Said I was. I didn't say anything to her. I bet she said I was acting strange.

"We all used to do weird things when we were kids, but it has to be something pretty serious for accusations of insanity being brought against us."

"Shut up. I don't know you."

Report back when I report back. Come down the hall and get me. Stop by my room. Don't you trust me? Yes, she came to see me with her hands in her eyes. I love you, Joseph. Inform me.

"What about your father?"

"He doesn't like me."

Reach up and touch my palm all the way up to my wrist get in a car and drive away. Silence there. Get inside me. Climb up in me. I'm worried. Run my fingers down her neck. I'm listening.

"Don't bring my father into it. He doesn't like me."

Worry in eyes that glance at you and feed you coffee. Insist that I'm thinking. Don't be nervous. Cut your nails down to the quick. Large eyes with dark lines under me. Ask me some questions why. He comes and spends almost three hours with me and questions me. Eyes in my belly.

Don't bring my father into me.

Ayesha, my Madonna I imagined before I saw you what you would mean. Eyes in my belly. Don't go away. Alone here, but it's not bad. A beard outside my window. Eudora when I raise my head. I pray looking upstairs.

Joseph made a mistake but I'm all well all right. A metamorphosis inside my head. I'm all ready to go. Sit down in their seat with them there's nothing I want to say to them.

"Are you all right, Joseph?"

"Yes, I'm. It's not cold in here why do you light the fire?"

Go into my closet but don't take me out. Things is good in here. The coats is warm.

"Are you too cold?"

"Naw. Feed me some coffee it will go down to my belly and I will be okay. Don't feel guilty. It's not bad in here. I keep saying prayers."

Yes Dora, yes Dora you mustn't feel sorry because I'm in here. Was. I don't drink coffee anymore. Bring me some Burgundy for dinner. I will sit on top of that little table and drink it because I'm changed.

Coffee in the living room settle yourself down over coffee.

"I didn't think you'd change."

"I don't like coffee anymore."

Laughing, laughter, it seems like a long time. I don't like any coffee please don't light me a cigarette I don't smoke puffs going all inside my head.

Trouble wouldn't come out I wouldn't come out and write you down all these things. Do you remember me? Yes, like all my visions. Discuss myself up to a point. Hold a grudge in my hand. Why don't you stay, Dora? No, because then you'd get worried. No.

Stay and hand me some wine. I'll wear a gray coat and grow me a mustache. What are you suspecting? Expecting? Alarm me with cookies, put tea in my belly. Calm so calm down in my belly potato chips and wine. That man with the bush that's my uncle but I know he's not. Strange feeling I got inside me.

Tell me something I expected that will make me feel good inside. Find out who I am.

Say something you are supposed to say to each other and find yourself a culture. Find yourself inside me somebody I'm telephoning to tell you who I am and go out my door. I hope the rain don't catch you. Fragmented water on my beard. It would please me very much if you would stay. Feed me tranquilizers and come in to see me.

Something I am doing something I am doing. Feed me my wine. I will run around without any clothes on so you will know who I am. Come inside me. Everyone will know and find me out. I wouldn't tell you. This is the way you see me. My eyes in the attic.

Come to confessional. You can do it inside your own head. I'm not an old man. Come inside and see what I believe vaguely, a purple chair. I can climb out your window only if I'm already inside. Come inside my house I will tell you who I am. I have become. Hands under Dora's skirt. Bad head I have a bad head fingers inside a book.

"Put your head in my lap."

"Naw."

Yes I'm tired find a pillow, an arm around me.

I don't want to become like Avrahm, my father. Wrap me up in myself. My words will work your magic. Are you starting to go? Yes, I know you. Everything you told me. I'll help you find your way out.